"Get out, oaf!" I [...] constable off. "I wou[...] [...] chit for all the money in the mint."

Lord Marndale looked quite stupefied, whether at my tone or the fact that I stood before him and his army in nothing but a nightgown, I do not know. I realized by his raking gaze at that point that I was undressed and grabbed my new silk dressing gown about me.

"Get this rabble out of here at once. At once, I say," I commanded, head high, eyes flashing.

Lord Marndale became aware of the rest of the audience and turned to the constable. "Thank you, officer. I can handle it from here."

"Will you be wanting manacles and a cell, milord?" the constable asked, subjecting me to a close examination.

"Don't be an ass," I said, shoving him out the door.

"A chair and a whip, perhaps . . ." Lord Marndale murmured, regarding me warily.

JENNIE
KISSED
ME

Joan Smith

FAWCETT CREST • NEW YORK

A Fawcett Crest Book
Published by Ballantine Books
Copyright © 1991 by Joan Smith

Library of Congress Catalog Card Number: 91-92196

ISBN 0-449-21844-9

Manufactured in the United States of America

First Edition: December 1991

Chapter One

"It wouldn't surprise me in the least," Mrs. Irvine declared, sliding her eyes to the couple standing at the far side of the desk. "It," the subject under discussion, was the probable lechery of the gentleman who had just entered the inn with a young lady. He was ordering rooms for the night and said bold as brass he would like adjoining chambers. "He wouldn't lay down his blunt for *two* chambers if they are married," Mrs. Irvine informed me.

"She's young enough to be his daughter," I objected.

"That's the way the gents like them, fresh and biddable."

Mrs. Irvine has picked up some strangely French notions in her travels. I, like any provincial greenhorn, took the gentleman for the young lady's husband. The reason for my displeasure was that such young ladies must nab all the eligible older gentlemen. This man looked to have a good ten years on my one score and seven. I, on the other hand, could give his bride a decade.

"I know a lightskirt to see one," Mrs. Irvine in-

1

sisted. "I recognize their tricks. You see she is not wearing a wedding ring."

I must digress a moment to explain how it comes that a perfectly respectable matron like Mrs. Irvine, niece to a dean and cousin to my respectable self, comes to be an expert on sexual misconduct. She is the widow of a naval captain, you see, and toured many parts of the world with him, which I think is explanation enough. Abroad she picked up tricks that would shock a seasoned courtesan. The reason we were loitering around the desk was that we had asked for a private parlor for dinner, and some minion was preparing one for us.

The young lady we were studying gave the man a brazen stare and said, "No! I shan't go to Wycherly with you, and that is that. You can't *make* me."

The gentleman insisted; she pouted; he begged; she sulked; finally he glared; she tossed her shoulders. "Wycherly is so boring," she complained. "Take me to Brighton. You promised you would."

"It is not Brighton he has in mind, but a feather tick," Mrs. Irvine whispered in my ear.

The gentleman's protestations went unheard but not unseen. From my vantage point at the other side of the desk, I studied him. His exquisite barbering alone was enough to peg him as a member of the ton. A glistening cap of black silk hair covered his well-shaped head. His face, alas, showed some signs of dissipation. Incipient wrinkles marked his weathered brow and crinkled the corners of his dark eyes. Annoyance deepened a pair of lines at the sides of his lips, but in his well-cut evening suit he was a handsome specimen. He towered a foot over the lady, and unless his shoulders were out of all proportion to the rest of his body, he was well built.

"He should try a diamond bracelet," Mrs. Irvine murmured. "That always worked with the lightskirts when I was young." The clerk lifted a brow and gave her a disparaging sniff.

I wished she would make clear to any chance listener that her experience was got at secondhand. She looked dowdy but perfectly respectable. In fact she looked exactly what she was: a Bath matron, complete with full figure, dark bonnet and pelisse, and sensible walking shoes. The gown beneath the pelisse defied dating. It belonged to no recognizable era or country. Ladies at sea lost touch with fashion, and now Mrs. Irvine had lost any interest in cutting a dash. Her swarthy complexion held the echoes of her life on the high seas. She is my first cousin once removed, which makes her a generation older than myself.

When I came unexpectedly into a fortune of ten thousand pounds from a nabob uncle I had never met, I threw up my job as school mistress in Mrs. Grambly's ladies' seminary in Bath, hired Mrs. Irvine as my companion, and set off for London. Mrs. Irvine, who has some tenuous connection with society, tells me ten thousand should buy me a baronet. It will be a baronet with an unencumbered estate and preferably a London house as well, or I will keep my blunt for myself.

So far as I am concerned, a husband is a desirable but dispensable accessory, like a diamond necklace or a sable-lined cape. He must be presentable-looking, amusing, and not too demanding of my time, if he wishes to get his hands on my fortune. I have no aversion to the single life so long as I don't have to spend it in front of a room full of chattering girls with a headmistress peering around the corner.

Of course, I realize that being a married lady would open more doors to amusement. In the past I have felt the burn of injustice, to receive letters from my former charges boasting of their marital conquests. No matter how ugly or stupid or ill-tempered, they all married so long as they had that essential dowry.

It was en route to the London Marriage Mart, at

the Laughing Jack Inn outside of Farnborough, that we encountered the couple under observation.

The gentleman was speaking. "I told you, Vickie, I cannot take you to Brighton at this time. My relatives would be in the boughs if I trotted in with you. You know I . . ." His voice petered into inaudibility, but the bit overheard was enough that I soon joined Mrs. Irvine in her opinion of the couple. Vickie continued pouting. Her escort gave some final, curt command and strode angrily away. Vickie was left alone at the desk, fuming.

"He picked up more than he bargained for in that one," Mrs. Irvine said. "She's better off without him. What she wants is some younger gent she can wind 'round her thumb. The older, stiffer ones don't wind so well."

"Poor thing, what will she do all alone here?" I asked. "We could offer her a lift back to London. At least I judge from that outfit that she is from London." Certainly nothing like her satin-lined pelisse had ever been seen in Bath. Her bonnet was a delightful confection with blue ribbons that just matched the lining.

"It won't do you any good to be seen entering town in company with a lightskirt, Jennie," Mrs. Irvine pointed out.

"Pooh. She looks perfectly respectable, and who will see us? We'll treat her to a bedroom tonight and drop her off wherever she wishes to go tomorrow. If this is her first patron, we might rehabilitate her."

Mrs. Irvine gave a jaundiced shake of her head. "She's not one of your respectable girls from a Bath seminary. That bit o' muslin has a mind of her own. I recommend caution."

"Oh, certainly!" I agreed, flying incautiously to the girl's side. Mrs. Irvine trailed along behind. At close range I had no reason to change my mind as to the lady's youth. She had the enviable, glossy eye of the very young, just on the verge of woman-

4

hood. Her skin was dewy, her teeth perfect. A rim of golden curls peeped from under the brim of the fashionable bonnet. Every instinct rebelled to think of that lecherous old man having his way with her.

I offered my hand, and after a surprised look she accepted it. "You must forgive me for interfering," I said. "I am Miss Robsjohn."

"I'm Victoria Savidge."

"The inn is busy tonight, is it not? My companion and I are waiting for a parlor. We are on our way from Bath to London. You are from London, I recollect?"

She gave a curious smile. "Why do you say that?"

"Because of your toilette. Very handsome, Miss Savidge."

"Thank you." She did not return any compliment on my new finery, but then one did not look for unexceptionable manners in a lightskirt. Her accent was good. Perhaps she was training up for the stage.

"I expect your . . . friend bought you the outfit? The gentleman who just pounced off in a huff."

She did not answer my question but said with a scowl, "He is so domineering there is no bearing it."

It was enough to encourage me to proceed. "I couldn't help overhearing your conversation just now. Mrs. Irvine and I would be happy to offer you a lift back to London."

Her luminous eyes held no lack of intelligence. Indeed crafty did not seem too strong a word to describe them. "But what should I tell my . . . friend?"

"Tell him nothing. Run while you have the chance. You should not have come here alone with a gentleman," I said. "It is unconscionable of that wretched man to have stalked off and left you stranded."

"Oh, but he will be back shortly," she said. "We were to stay here the night." Her head turned to the front door. The gentleman was indeed back, even earlier than we both liked. Miss Victoria scowled. I returned his stare as he paused a moment to glare at me then pelted swiftly forward.

"Come along, Vickie," he said sharply, and placed a commanding hand on her wrist. Vickie wrenched away. You would think Mrs. Irvine and myself were a pair of thieves, the black look he gave us. It was a thoroughly insulting, contemptuous look. I returned bold stare for stare. He grabbed Vickie's wrist again and stalked toward the staircase, dragging the girl after him. Vickie looked helplessly over her shoulder. My blood ran cold to think of that innocent young thing helpless in a room with this anonymous lecher.

"A moment, sir!" I called in a voice loud enough to command the attention of the half-dozen bodies in the lobby. "Miss Victoria has changed her mind. She is coming to London with me." I advanced to rescue her from his clutches.

His glare turned from me to Victoria. "Must you take up with every hedgebird who comes along?" he asked her, making no effort to lower his voice.

"You are mistaken, sir. No doubt you are judging Miss Victoria's eagerness to collect hedgebirds from her association with yourself. My companion and I are perfectly respectable."

His dark eyes raked us from head to toe. "That is a matter of opinion," he retaliated, and resumed his trip toward the staircase. I felt Mrs. Irvine's fingers tugging at my elbow and shook her off.

There was nothing for it but to go after them. "Unhand that girl, if you don't want me to call in the law," I threatened.

The man's face turned from pink to purple. "Go to hell, madam," he said, and started climbing the stairs. I caught hold of his coattail and hung on till he was forced to stop.

"You ought to be ashamed of yourself. That child is young enough to be your daughter."

"For your information, miss, she *is* my daughter," he growled, and wrenched his coat from my fingers. Shock left them perfectly useless. My eyes fled to Victoria, who gave an insouciant, smiling shrug of agreement over her shoulder as they proceeded in state up the stairs. I looked down to the lobby and saw a circle of smirking faces having a good laugh at my expense.

"A likely story!" I called up after their retreating forms.

The inn clerk came mincing forward. "Aye, 'tis true. That there is the Marquess of Marndale and his daughter, Lady Victoria. They live twenty-five mile yonder, at Wycherly Park."

"If you mean twenty-five miles, say so," I sniffed, and strode, cheeks flaming, head high, back down to the lobby. "Is our private parlor ready yet, or have you been too busy eavesdropping on conversations that don't concern you to attend to it?"

"Your parlor's free now, madam," he smirked, and led Mrs. Irvine and myself, sunk to utter humiliation, into a cozy room. The fire burned briskly. Normally its warmth would have been welcome in late April, but I felt no need for more heat on that occasion. I was blushing all over from shame. "A bottle of wine while we await dinner, please," I said to the clerk.

"I'll send you a servant, madam," he replied with a sneer. What did he think he was? The Archbishop of Canterbury?

"Well," Mrs. Irvine said, with that "I told you so" look, "You can't say I didn't warn you to use a little caution."

My temper broke. "That wretched girl! Why didn't she *tell* me he was her father? Surely she understood my meaning when I spoke of not being alone with him."

"She's a minx, and he's got Old Nick's own temper. We want to stay clear of them when we're leav-

7

ing. As he's hired rooms, it seems they are remaining overnight, thank God."

I sank onto a chair and dissolved in a puddle of shame. It was only a cruel stroke of chance that brought us to this inn at all. Our itinerary, which I had worked out in meticulous detail, called for us to spend the night in Farnborough, where I had arranged by post to have a bed awaiting us. We had planned to take dinner there as well, but between slow horses, ravening hunger, and general boredom, we decided to take dinner at the Laughing Jack and go on to Farnborough to sleep.

"I hope I never have to see him again as long as I live," I said wearily. "Thank God he is taking her to Wycherly and not to London."

"If he's anybody, he'll be going on to London for the Season," my Job's Comforter assured me. "Not that we're likely to meet him. My connections are not high and mighty marquesses. A knight or a baronet is the best I can hope to do for you. If you wish to disgrace yourself in front of marquesses, you'll have to arrange it yourself."

"I have admitted you urged caution and I did not heed your advice, Mrs. Irvine. Don't make a meal of my error."

When our wine came we ordered dinner, and over a mutton chop and a raised pigeon pie we discussed the incident less emotionally. "He must have married young," I mentioned. "He did not look more than thirty-six or -seven, did you think? And Victoria must be sixteen or seventeen."

"He could have married at twenty, I suppose. Odd his wife is not travelling with him."

"Perhaps he's a widower," I said idly. "What is odder is that he should have been telling his own daughter he could not take her to Brighton. Some relatives he gave as the excuse, did he not?" Mrs. Irvine nodded indifferently. "She didn't correct me

8

when I called her Miss Savidge. I begin to think he is shamming the waiter with that story."

Mrs. Irvine is but an indifferent conversationalist when she is eating. No matter that the meal was wretched. The chop was of bullet-proof consistency and the gravy so thick you had to cut it with a knife. She made some vague and incomprehensible sound and put another bite of pie into her mouth, which left me alone with my shame and my questions. Mrs. Irvine felt that if she had two desserts, she would not require more food at Farnborough, and to avoid another meal I went along with her. It was an hour after we entered the parlor that we finally left and went to our carriage. With the smirking eyes of the inn upon us, we carried our noses high, like a pair of camels.

Farnborough, our driver told me, was eight miles farther along, not two as originally thought. With an hour to kill, Mrs. Irvine and I curled up in the carriage, pulled a blanket over us, and prepared to pass the hour in idle conversation, mostly about our recent embarrassment.

We shared one banquette in the dark carriage. We had been travelling for two days and had managed to fill one side of the seating space with a miscellany of items to pass the time. Magazines, a box of bonbons, a spare shawl, Mrs. Irvine's netting basket, with a spare blanket thrown over it all. Neither of us gave a second glance at the dark hump in the corner. It was silent and unmoving. How should we suspect a mischievous human body was concealed beneath the blanket?

My first intimation of disaster occurred when Mrs. Irvine dozed off to sleep. From her life on the high sea, she bragged, she could sleep on an active threshing machine. She kept pulling the blanket around her, leaving me uncovered and chilly. Rather than disturb her I reached across and seized

9

the other blanket. And still I did not realize what I had uncovered. She had her face hidden, you see, and her dark pelisse looked like Mrs. Irvine's spare shawl. It was that sixth sense that finally alerted me. There was an eerie sensation of another presence. I felt a shiver over my scalp. I stared at the dark hump, and as we turned a corner a wan moonbeam picked out the configuration of a human hand.

I let out a shriek to wake the dead, and that is when Lady Victoria sat up straight. "Don't be frightened. It's only me," she laughed. "You said I might go to London with you."

Mrs. Irvine awoke with a start. "What? What?" Her shrieks were added to mine.

"It's Lady Victoria," I told her.

"Good gracious. So it is. I thought we were being boarded by pirates at least." She leaned forward eagerly. "Tell the truth now, missie. That man at the inn is not your papa, is he?"

"Certainly he is," she answered.

"Why can he not take you to Brighton? He mentioned some relatives . . ."

"My great-aunts think I should still be in school—at *my* age!"

"And what age is that, dear?"

"Nearly seventeen."

I was the unwitting kidnapper of a noble sixteen-year-old lady, whose papa had the devil's own temper.

"There'll be the father and mother of a row when he discovers you've slipped overboard. I'd stake my head on it," Mrs. Irvine said with satisfaction. I knew she found life dull since parting company with pirates and wild Indians and shipwrecks.

"We must get you back to him at once!" I declared weakly. Across the miles I could feel his dark eyes burn into me, and I felt a horrible presentiment of chaos to follow.

"Did you not mean your kind offer to help me?" Lady Victoria pouted.

"It was a misunderstanding. We thought you were his *chère amie*," Mrs. Irvine confided. Lady Victoria laughed delightedly. I glared futilely in the darkness of the carriage.

"Oh, here we are at Farnborough," she said a moment later. "Papa won't miss me till morning. He thinks I am asleep. I put some pillows under the blankets to fool him.

"Aboard the *Prometheus*, we used to use the ship's dog for that stunt," Mrs. Irvine informed this innocent young schoolgirl. "Then you have a hairy head on the pillow if the husband comes looking. You want to be sure to feed the dog ale first, for dogs are so jumpy. Old Walsenby had the shock of his life when his 'wife' leapt up and started licking him one night."

Glancing out I saw the myriad lighted windows of the city spread before us. With our inn so close at hand, it seemed a good idea to continue on there and decide what was best to be done. Our team was winded, and to return our unwelcome guest we would have to hire fresh horses. Within five minutes the carriage was lumbering into the coaching yard of a half-timbered inn, and we three ladies alit. Lady Victoria smiled unconcernedly and hung onto my arm as though I were her escort.

"You must be sure to tell your father this was your idea. We had no notion you were with us," I pointed out firmly.

"But it *was* your idea, Miss Robsjohn. You invited me."

She smiled blandly, and I, with great effort, suppressed the urge to box her noble ears.

Chapter Two

Mrs. Irvine got her second meal after all. We retired to a private parlor to discuss what we should do, and as we were entertaining a noble lady, I asked for wine. Mrs. Irvine requested sandwiches to accompany it, and Lady Victoria thought she could eat a few macaroons and perhaps a cream bun.

"We must get you back before your father misses you," I said firmly to Lady Victoria. After insisting on the macaroons, she didn't touch them but ploughed into the cream bun as if it were manna from heaven.

"He won't miss me till morning."

"I shall ask the inn to rent me a fresh team and take her back at once. I suppose we could not send her alone." I spoke aside to Mrs. Irvine. "I must own, I do not relish the prospect of meeting Lord Marndale again."

"We cannot send a young lady pelting about the countryside without a chaperone at night. He'd never see a hair of her head. She'd head straight for London. You'll have to go with her, Jennie."

"Bother! *We* will have to go with her."

"Lord, my poor bones cannot take anymore shaking this night. What do you say we send him a note and tell him he may collect her here?"

I had developed a menial attitude from my working past. I was happy Mrs. Irvine alerted me to it. "Perfect! Why should *we* have the bother of the trip, when *he* is the one who let her escape? I'll ask for paper and write the note at once for John Groom to deliver."

I rang the bell and wrote the note. There was no cringing or grovelling in it. I said brusquely that Lady Victoria had concealed herself in my carriage without my knowledge or consent, and gave directions for him to pick her up. The instant it was done I sent it off, asking my driver to hire a mount and go on horseback to save time.

"Less than half an hour to get the note to Lord Marndale, and an hour for him to reach us," I said. "We may as well wait here. We don't want to be in our nightgowns when he comes."

That left ninety minutes, more or less, to discover what we could of our runaway. We put the time to good use.

"Your mama is at Wycherly Park, is she?" I asked.

"Mama died when I was born," Lady Victoria said, looking up from her cream bun with a long face. A daub of cream on her chin quite ruined her pose. She wished to give herself the airs of an abandoned orphan, when she had obviously been raised in the very lap of luxury.

"Lord Marndale scarcely looks old enough to be your father," Mrs. Irvine mentioned.

"He married my mother when she was seventeen and he, nineteen. They were childhood sweethearts, living right next door. He has never remarried."

13

"That's a long time to be without a woman. I expect he has lady friends?" I need scarcely identify the speaker as Mrs. Irvine.

"Oh, yes. Many ladies throw their hankies at him, but he is interested in politics now. He spends a deal of time in London. Perhaps he has a mistress there. At least he never wants me to go with him, though I shall next year to make my debut. Could I have another cream bun, Miss Robsjohn, please?"

I rang the bell and ordered another cream bun and tea. Eating was better than drinking an excess of wine. I didn't want her bosky when her father came for her.

"Did you attend a ladies' seminary, Lady Victoria?" I asked, to pass the time.

"No, I had a governess. Miss Clancy married a neighboring tutor last month, which is why I was visiting Aunt Clara in Salisbury till Papa could come home. To Wycherly Park, I mean. He has been in London. I was supposed to remain with Aunt Clara till August, when we were to go to Brighton." She added in a pouting way, "I don't see why we cannot go now if he won't let me go to London."

"And why did you leave your Aunt Clara early?" Mrs. Irvine inquired. Her coy look suggested sexual carrying-on.

Lady Victoria hunched her elegant shoulders. "I expect it was because of Mr. Borsini, the Italian singing instructor. As if I would have run off with *him*! We were only sitting in the conservatory while he helped me with my Italian grammar lessons."

I began to feel a twinge of pity for Lord Marndale. "There is something to be said for sending ladies to a seminary," I told her, and outlined my own past career.

"Good gracious, you mean you're a teacher!" she exclaimed, studying my toilette. "I took you for a lady."

"I *am* a lady!" I replied, high on my dignity.

I glanced in the mirror over the grate to reassure myself on that score. Certainly I looked every inch the lady in my new finery, acquired since coming into my inheritance. How thrilled I had been to discard my ugly round bonnets and severe dark gowns. I now wore what was the highest kick of fashion in Bath society, but Lady Victoria's toilette put me in the shade. For travelling my outfit consisted of a dark green worsted suit with a fichu of Belgian lace at the neck. My figure was more athletic than feminine, but with, of course, some indication between the neck and knees that I was a woman. I have a noticeable waist is what I mean, with some fullness above it. My travelling bonnet was plain but worn with a dashing tilt over the eye.

I removed the bonnet for greater comfort and because my hair is my crowning glory. It is a true Titian red and gives a clue to my short temper, which made me such a successful purveyor of knowledge to youngsters. They did not trifle with Miss Robsjohn. Since I am no longer required to be a dragon, however, I am endeavoring to sweeten my astringent disposition. I smiled at the reflection in the mirror.

Mr. Vivaldi, Bath's reigning coiffeur, had achieved a splendid do for me. How happy I was to have that eternal knob lobbed off and let my natural curl have its way. I wear my hair short and saucy, because, quite frankly, it removes a few of my seven and twenty years. Dare I try to pass myself off as twenty-four? There is something so terribly irrevocable about being past the quarter-century mark! Yes, I would be twenty-four when I reached London, which would require a clever memory not to mention I had been teaching for six years. Three years, I would say. My eyes would not give me away in any case. They are green; not so

15

lustrous as Lady Victoria's, but no crow's-feet have left their calling card at the corners.

My nose is severely straight, with no entrancing tilt at the end like my guest's. My jaw is firm, but at least my teeth are in good repair. I would never play the ingenue again, but I would not be a spinster either, nor one notch below a perfect lady. I caught Mrs. Irvine's eagle eye watching me admiring myself and turned back to the company.

"You are on your way to Wycherly Park with your father now, are you, Lady Victoria?" You must not think I was in the least intimidated by her title! I dealt with any number of noble girls at the seminary, which meant some rubbing of shoulders with their parents as well. One young lady was under the guardianship of her bachelor brother, Lord Anselm. I do not say he made a point of attending every open day for the sole purpose of seeing me, but he did hint on a few occasions that he enjoyed our meetings.

"Only until he can find someone else to look after me. Aunt Clara warned Cousin Eugenia that I would be too much for her, so I expect it will be another governess. No, *companion*," she said. "I am too old for a governess."

Why could a position like this not have come along when I had to work for a living? I used to scan the papers daily for some such sinecure. But it was academic now. "Perhaps I could put you on to someone," I said, mentally fingering Miss Hopkins for the post. She was my greatest friend amongst the teaching staff at the seminary. A genteel-born, penniless lady like myself. I doubted she would have the fortitude to handle Lady Victoria, however. Especially if a continental teaching master formed any part of the household.

I inquired about this and was told that Lady Victoria was finished with all instruction. Borsini was her Aunt Clara's idea. I would mention Lydia Hopkins to Lord Marndale. It would be pleasant to share my new happiness with an old friend, and I would keep in touch with Lady Victoria's progress through Lydia. I had a feeling that Lady Victoria's future would provide interesting reading.

My guest took exactly one bite of the second cream bun, heedless of the cost, which would be put on my bill. "I'm tired. I would like to go to bed now," she announced.

"Your father should be here inside of an hour," I pointed out. "It is not worthwhile getting undressed."

"But it's nearly eleven o'clock. I go to bed at ten."

"Lie down on the settee," I suggested. "I'll get a bolster for you."

"I cannot sleep on that!"

Given the choice of sitting on a hard chair or resting on the settee, she soon chose the latter. She occupied the entire couch, making it necessary for Mrs. Irvine and myself to use the hard chairs. Before long the girl was sleeping. I got a blanket to put over her, and Mrs. Irvine and I talked for as long as we could keep our eyes open. At midnight our driver tapped at the door. He had left my note for Lord Marndale but had not spoken to him.

"Why did you not request a meeting?" I demanded, shocked at such a desultory attitude. Mrs. Irvine had procured our driver for us. I knew nothing about the man, except that he seemed a good-enough whip for someone who had spent his adult years aboard a ship.

"You said deliver the note. I delivered it."

"You did not deliver it to Lord Marndale."

"He was aboard. The lad at the desk said he would see that his lordship got it. Never worry your head about it, missie. He'll be here before you're ready to cast off."

17

Mrs. Irvine began yawning into her fist and suggested we "hit our bunks." "Lord Marndale will be here any moment. He would have a fast team," I countered.

At twelve-thirty she suggested it again. I was angry enough to consider it, but surely he could not be much longer. At one o'clock I agreed. Obviously something had gone amiss. Lord Marndale must have stepped out to visit friends, or was in a drunken stupor for all I knew. I left a message for him at the desk, explaining where he could find his daughter. We woke Lady Victoria, and all three of us went up to the single room I had hired. The inn provided us a truckle bed for our guest.

I lent Lady Victoria my best lawn nightie, which she took without even saying thank you. Then she just stood there like a statue, waiting for me to undress her.

"Be sure you hang up your gown," I said, and undressed myself.

She gave me a sulky look but managed to get out of her gown and into the nightie and even hung up her clothes. Her next imposition was to hop into my bed.

"I shouldn't think the three of us will fit in there," I said. "The truckle bed is for you, Lady Victoria."

"But I can't sleep in that rickety little thing," she laughed.

"It will be better than the floor, don't you think?" I assisted her out of my bed and nodded to Mrs. Irvine to hop in against the wall. I took the other place and watched with amusement while Lady Victoria examined the truckle bed. She walked around it three times, like a dog around his blanket, then climbed in.

"It's lumpy," she complained.

"You will want to remember all these inconveniences before you run away again," I told her.

"You're right. You *are* a lady," was the last phrase she spoke.

I pondered her meaning for all of five minutes before my mind wandered off to more interesting matters. What could be delaying Lord Marndale? What never entered my mind was that he had called out the constable and sent a crew out scouring the roads for us. The first intimation of that delightful surprise occurred at three o'clock in the morning, when I was awakened by a loud pounding at the door.

Chapter Three

I leapt from the bed in terror and lit the taper, calling "Who is it?" In my dazed state I envisaged a blackguard with pistol and knife ready to rob and kill me. The pounding drowned out my voice. The next thing I knew fists gave way to a battering ram, and someone began hammering the door down with a piece of heavy furniture. Surely a thief in the night would not be so brazen! I spotted Victoria on the truckle bed and knew my caller was no thief. Worse, it was Lord Marndale.

After three or four assaults the door remained intact, but the lock gave way. Lord Marndale was accompanied by a veritable army of minions, some in livery, some in fustian, and one wearing a constable's hat. His lordship's temper was hot enough to burn the shell off an egg. His hair fell over his forehead, perspiration dripped from his brow, and the stuffing from the chair he was using as a battering ram left a film of brown dust on his evening suit. The elegant marquess looked for the world as if he had robbed a scarecrow of his jacket. He dropped the chair with a loud thump and pointed a finger at me. "Arrest that woman, officer. She has abducted my daughter."

The foolish constable came blundering forward, stumbling over the chair at the doorway, and took hold of my arm. The racket had roused the other patrons, who stuck their heads from their various doors. Men in nightcaps, ladies with their hair in rags, and one gleaming bald scalp popped out like cuckoos from a row of clocks, all goggling at my room. The scene was too ludicrous to inspire terror. "Get out, oaf!" I said, and shook the constable off. "I wouldn't kidnap that bold chit for all the money in the mint."

Mrs. Irvine and Lady Victoria were awakened by the commotion and joined their shrieks to the general mêlée. My lungs, strengthened from long holding forth in the classroom, could be heard above the hubbub. I turned a fiery eye on Lord Marndale. "It is about time you got here, sir."

He ignored me and rushed to the truckle bed to draw his daughter into his arms. I heard tender outpourings, asking the hussy if she was all right and if we had harmed her. My temper was up at his attitude, and I went after him. "*Harmed* her?" I demanded.

To escape her papa's wrath, or perhaps just from a love of attention, she burst into tears. "It was horrid," she gasped. "And only look where she is making me sleep, Papa, in this horrid cot."

"This is outrageous!" Lord Marndale exclaimed, rising to turn on me like a virago.

"Indeed it is, sir. It is outrageous that your daughter hid herself in my carriage and has battened herself on me quite shamelessly, causing me no end of bother and expense. I have sat up half the night waiting for you to come and retrieve her, to say nothing of her ordering expensive food which she did not eat. If you think for one moment I was

21

about to be put out of my bed as well, you have another think coming."

Lord Marndale looked quite stupefied, whether at my tone or the fact that I stood before him and his army in nothing but a nightgown, I do not know. I realized by his raking gaze at that point that I was undressed and grabbed my new silk dressing gown about me. It is a charming peacock blue color, with a long fringed sash and notched lapels, like a gentleman's jacket.

"Get this rabble out of here at once. At once, I say," I commanded, head high, eyes flashing.

Lord Marndale became aware of the rest of the audience and turned to the constable. "Thank you, officer. I can handle it from here."

"Will you be wanting manacles and a cell, milord?" the constable asked, subjecting me to a close examination.

"Don't be an ass," I said, shoving him out the door.

"A chair and a whip, perhaps ..." Lord Marndale murmured, regarding me warily.

I slammed the door, thus lowering the curtain on the night's entertainment for the audience.

Lord Marndale looked surprised though not greatly so. "Now perhaps you will do me the honor of explaining what you are doing with my daughter, madam, after I explicitly told you to mind your own business," he said loftily.

"That is precisely what I am trying to do. I did not abduct her, and I would thank you to tell your constable so. She concealed herself in my carriage. I didn't know she was there till we had nearly reached Farnborough."

"At what time was that?"

"After ten."

"Then you have had ample time to return her."

"Yes, sir, I had the time but not the inclination to subject my elderly companion to further jostling after dark." Mrs. Irvine sniffed at being called elderly, but she sniffed in Lord Marndale's direction. "I sent a note off to you at once. I have been waiting to hear from you for hours."

"I wasn't at the inn. As soon as I discovered Victoria was missing, I raised the alarm and went out looking for her."

"Then it is strange you did not find her, as you knew I was en route to London and apparently had fingered me as the culprit."

"I discovered you were from Bath. They mentioned it at the inn. I thought London was dust in my eyes."

I gave an incredulous snort. "Surely dust in the eyes of a blind man is redundant."

"What was I to think?" he demanded in a loud voice. He lowered a slash of black eyebrows into a scowl, to try to intimidate me. "You had been trying to lure her away. Are you abbesses so short of girls you have taken to scouring the countryside for innocent maidens?"

I was not aware at the time of the slanderous meaning of the term "abbess," but Mrs. Irvine, of course, was privy to it and called him to account. "Now see here, you jackdaw, who are you calling brothel keepers?" she demanded. "I'll have you know Jennie is a school mistress, and I am a decent widow. It's a rake like yourself who knows all about abbesses."

"Then why were you trying to lure Victoria away at the inn?"

"That was a misunderstanding," I rushed in. "Your daughter will tell you. . . . "

The minx let her lower lip tremble. "It was partly my fault, Papa," she said. "They didn't beat me." I could only stare at her lukewarm commendation.

"Did you conceal yourself in Miss Robsjohn's carriage, Victoria?" he asked her.

I assumed he had got my name from the inn, as well as my city of origin. "Yes, Papa," she said, gazing at him with those big eyes where tears were gathering adorably.

Lord Marndale took himself by the scruff of the neck and braced himself to do something he obviously found extremely difficult. He apologized. "I must beg your pardon, Miss Robsjohn. It seems I have wronged you. In my anxiety I went ripping off without thinking what I was about. I am wretchedly sorry."

I wanted only to have done with the whole unseemly business. "Next time you will know where to lay the blame," I said, with an icy glance at his wayward daughter. "And perhaps you will even recognize a lady the next time you meet one."

"Victoria, you will apologize to Miss Robsjohn," he ordered.

"Sorry, ma'am," she said with a playful curtsy.

"You are forgiven. No harm done. You had best get dressed, Lady Victoria. Your father will take care of you now."

"What she wants is a good thrashing," Mrs. Irvine advised. "Keelhauling is too good for her."

Lord Marndale ignored her and turned to me. "Naturally I wish to reimburse you for any undue expense you have incurred," he said.

The price of a plate of uneaten macaroons and two cream buns hardly seemed worth bothering with. "It was nothing."

"But she shared your room."

"The cost of a truckle bed is negligible, I assure you. Perhaps you will wait outside while your daughter changes. I promise you we will not sneak her out the window." I didn't mean to let her away in my best lawn nightie. He left, and Lady Victoria gave me a sheepish smile. "I am sorry, Miss Robsjohn," she said.

"Mrs. Irvine has also been inconvenienced by your stunt," I said coldly. She apologized to Mrs. Irvine as well.

"Oh, that's all right. It was quite exciting, having men bursting into our room. Quite like old times," my irrepressible companion smiled.

"Mrs. Irvine was in the navy," I heard myself say. It didn't seem worthwhile to explain further. I glared Mrs. Irvine into silence and helped Lady Victoria dress. Inside of ten minutes she was presentable. I opened the door and found Lord Marndale leaning against the far wall with his arms crossed. He had combed his hair and made some attempt to remove the dirt from his jacket. He came forward, full of more apologies.

"This is very kind of you. I am indeed sorry for all the bother my daughter has caused. I'll speak to you later, Victoria," he added, with a cross glance at her. She looked fairly bored at his threat.

"The sooner the better," I told him.

"Daughters this age are the very devil, especially when they have no mother."

I ignored that blatant bid for sympathy. "All the more reason for their fathers to keep their wits about them, *n'est-ce pas*?"

"A hit. A palpable hit!" He smiled and crossed his arms, as if planning to linger a while.

I noticed that his eyes were roving with interest over my tousled hair and dressing gown. It was an unnerving experience, especially after his talk of abbesses. This man was no stranger to lightskirts, to judge by the assessing light in his eyes.

I yanked my dressing gown more tightly around me and said cooly, "It is nearly morning."

Lord Marndale apologized once again and said good night. I closed the door and drew a deep sigh. "Well, that is that. Fancy that bold chit saying we had not beaten her, as though we had done every other horrible thing imaginable. And her father is as bad."

"Worse!"

25

"You didn't have to make such a Judy of yourself, calling him a rake.'

"He oughtn't to have called *me* an abbess."

"Well, he is a marquess, you know, and they feel the world is theirs. You probably hurt his feelings."

"You couldn't hurt his feelings with a hatchet. I know his sort."

My working mentality still clung to me. This awe of the upper classes had to be beaten down before I got to London. "He was checking up on me, Mrs. Irvine," I scolded. "Asking where I was from."

"That's the only sensible move he did make. If you had any children of your own, you'd know how upset he was."

"You don't have any children. What makes you an expert?"

"We *elderly* ladies have seen much of the world," she replied, with a rebuking look at my former description.

"I only said it to justify not taking her back to the inn. Not that I feel I did wrong in writing to him instead! I expect we will be the talk of this inn by morning. So pleasant to look forward to."

We talked a little longer about the incident. "We've kicked this horse to death. Let us hit the tick," Mrs. Irvine said.

We returned to our beds and eventually to sleep. As I dozed off it darted into my head that if by any chance we happened to come across Lord Marndale in London there would be no cause for embarrassment on my side. The shoe was on the other foot now. If he was a gentleman, he ought really to repay my kindness to his daughter in some manner. A trip to the theater, perhaps, or a drive in the park. But then it was unlikely we would meet him. Where was such high society to be found, I wondered.

As events turned out, we encountered the marquess and his daughter long before we got to London. But first I had the remainder of a night's sleep.

Chapter Four

When the inn servant brought us our hot water in the morning, she handed me a note. *Marndale!* was, of course, the first thing that flashed into my head. I opened the note and read with amazement an invitation for me and my companion to join him belowstairs in his private parlor for breakfast. I showed the note to Mrs. Irvine. "Surely he has not come to Farnborough this early in the morning just to thank us again."

She was as astonished as myself but more logical. "More likely they stayed here overnight. It was pretty late to be taking his daughter back to the Laughing Jack."

This, while less flattering to me, made eminent good sense. He knew we must meet downstairs, and by asking us to be his guests he was repaying any social obligation the breaking down of our door and calling us names entailed. I would have preferred to have the debt paid in London but sent down an answer that we would join him shortly. Next followed the important decision of what to wear. As we were travelling, it must be something fairly utilitarian. I had earmarked my green serge for travel and put it on again.

"Don't mention the navy, Mrs. Irvine," I said as we went below. This was understood between us to mean she should not chatter too familiarly about the conduct of our Tars when ashore.

"Don't get your tail up your back," she riposted. "I know how to talk to a gentleman."

Lord Marndale was hovering at the door of his private parlor and came forward the minute we hit the bottom of the stairs. All the ravages of travel and door battering were removed from his toilette. As he wore a jacket of Bath cloth and a fresh cravat, I assumed his valet was on hand to assist him. "Miss Robsjohn, Mrs. Irvine," he said, making a graceful bow while he smiled civilly. This new expression removed the air of a savage from him. He was a handsome specimen when he wore civil manners. "So kind of you to join me."

Mrs. Irvine curtsied; I offered my hand. Mrs. Grambly once scolded me for shaking hands with a gentleman at the seminary. She said it was out of place in a schoolmistress, as it suggested equality with the parents of our students. I hoped Lord Marndale was aware of its significance. I inquired for Lady Victoria.

"My daughter is still resting," he explained. "I have coffee waiting for us." He lifted one finger, literally—his small finger at that—and a waiter came running to see what we would like with our coffee.

I don't know how it is, but I am always as hungry as a horse when travelling. At home I never take more than bread and tea in the morning, but on the road I eat like an infantryman. Like Lord Marndale, I ordered gammon and eggs. He apologized

28

again, and as we tackled our food he stated his real reason for inviting us.

"As you perhaps know, I am taking my daughter home to Wycherly Park. It is only a few miles out of your way. I would be delighted if you ladies would do me the honor of joining us for luncheon there."

I could not have been more surprised if he had asked me to marry him. Surely this was more civility than either our kindness to his daughter or his insults required. It looked like a real overture at friendship. His whole manner was so engaging, his conversation easy and accompanied by an indefinable air of what I can only call admiration when he looked at me. At the school the parents spoke to us teachers as if we were somehow less than human. They did not really look at us. I always felt they could not tell if my eyes were blue or green or red after they walked out the door. But if staring meant anything, Marndale could tell you not only their color, but how many lashes were on my eyelids.

The friendship of a marquess could not do a young lady any harm in her search for a husband in London. It seemed the doors of society might open wide enough for me to squeak in if I played my cards right. I must not be too eager; on the other hand, I had every intention of accepting.

To my dismay I heard Mrs. Irvine say, "Very kind, Lord Marndale, but Jennie has us on a rigid schedule. We must reach London by tonight. She has arranged our rooms in advance all along the route. Tonight we have rooms waiting at Rendall's Hotel."

Her reply annoyed me on several scores. I had no intention of being "Jennie," in London. Jennie is a fit name for a cow, not a lady. All this talk of rigid schedules made me sound a dead bore, and worst of all she had announced our destination as the second-rate Rendall's Hotel. Such eminences as Lord Marndale would put up at Claridge's or the Pulteney. Yet to refute her would sound like unbridled eagerness.

"You could still make it, if you spring your horses," he said. "Wycherly Park is worth a visit, if it is not immodest in me to say so. It is in all the guidebooks."

Before Mrs. Irvine could announce the ineligibility of "springing" the sort of job horses we managed to hire, I spoke up. "How far away is Wycherly Park, Lord Marndale?"

"Just a little jog south of Woking—practically on your way."

"We have to stop for luncheon, Mrs. Irvine," I pointed out to my recalcitrant friend.

Lord Marndale spoke on of his house, luring us with tales of its historical associations and physical features. He harped quite a while on the parks and gardens, done by Capability Brown in the last century.

"You might as well save your breath to cool your porridge, my lord," Mrs. Irvine said. "You will never get Jennie to change her plans. It comes from being a school teacher, I suppose. She is all for keeping to our schedule. I wanted to stop over a day at Devizes. There was a fellow putting on a raree-show, but she wouldn't hear of messing up our schedule." Lord Marndale's jaw fell open in astonishment.

"You make me sound a Tartar, Mrs. Irvine," I objected, casting a menacing eye on her. "What will Lord Marndale think to hear his estate compared to a raree-show? I should like of all things to see Wycherly Park. We accept your invitation, sir."

He expressed his pleasure, then said, "So you were a schoolmistress, Miss Robsjohn?" in a way that asked for elucidation.

I gave him the bare facts of my residence at the Bath Seminary, beginning as a junior assistant at the same school I had attended when my father was alive. The actual number of years spent there was not pinpointed. He said he had relatives who sent their daughters there, and we discussed the young ladies in question till breakfast was over. He was too polite to inquire how I had suddenly become wealthy enough to desert my career, and I did not volunteer the information. A touch of mystery, I felt, might make me an object of some interest. Before leaving it was arranged that our driver should follow Lord Marndale's carriage to Wycherly.

I had a hasty word with my John Groom, advising him to hire the fastest team possible, for I did not wish to look a complete flat in front of Lord Marndale. I could not but feel the disparity in our rigs, however, when he and Lady Victoria went out to their sleek chariot with the lozenge on the door, pulled by four matched bays. My poor old second-hand cart looked like the relic it was, and I had not thought to tell John Groom to hire four nags.

"I'll set a slow pace so you can keep up with us," I heard Marndale tell my groom.

Lady Victoria showed no pleasure or interest that we were going to Wycherly. I assumed her father had chastised her, for she was subdued and polite.

The detour south to Wycherly occurred just west of Woking. We drove for a little over an hour with Mrs. Irvine telling me every five minutes that we would never make London by nightfall but we would have to pay for our room all the same since we had asked them at Rendall's to hold it.

"What if we do?" I asked. "The price of one night's lodging won't break us. You must realize, Mrs. Irvine, that Lord Marndale could be a very helpful social ally in London, if he chose to take us up."

31

"You're flying too high, Jennie. He is just being polite. Very likely he is treating us today so he won't have to have anything to do with us in London. Gentlemen like to pay off their debts."

"That is news to me." I felt she had hit it on the head and was furious with the bearer of bad tidings. "You are becoming cynical in your old age. I think I prefer your naval mode. I am surprised you haven't claimed he is trying to seduce me."

"I wouldn't put it past him, but he wouldn't do it with his daughter in tow. He thinks too much of her. For ravishing women, men use an inn, usually in the country."

We were certainly in the deep country here. We drove through hill and hollow, with carefully tended fields where varying shades of green suggested the market and nursery crops under cultivation in the fertile brick-earth of the Thames valley. It was an ever-changing landscape. We passed through areas where tree followed tree, catching glimpses of cattle grazing beyond. Clouds of flowering wild bushes bosomed the hillsides, lending an air of enchantment. I knew from my teaching books that the North Downs must be close by. Before we reached them Lord Marndale's carriage turned in at a pair of wrought-iron gates and continued along a drive of crushed stone into what must have been Capability Brown's park.

It was too beautiful to be natural. Nature gives us a more ragged sort of beauty. Here clumps of trees were artfully arranged to give interesting vistas. At a turn in the drive the main building suddenly loomed before us like a mountain. It was of gray stone, the façade plain to the point of severity. Two stories had long windows with a third row of smaller windows forming the attics, or servants' quarters, above. The long roofline was punctuated only by chimneys. There were no domes or turrets, no statues or other embellishments. Were it not for the delightful setting, it would have looked like an institution.

John Groom drew to a stop behind Lord Marndale's carriage, and we alit for a closer look at the grounds. Lush grass provided a green carpet as far as the eye could see. In the distance water gleamed in the sunlight, curving sinuously as a snake. A bulge here and there was bordered with blooming bushes. At other points huge stone pots on columns met the eye. A few graceful willows trailed their branches at the water's edge to vary the scene.

"Welcome to Wycherly Park," Lord Marndale said with an echo of pride in his accent. He offered his arm, adding, "We'll go in and have some refreshment."

I expressed my admiration of the grounds. Mrs. Irvine yawned and stretched and pointed to a little hump in the grass. "You have moles. You want to get after them, Lord Marndale," was her compliment on all his grandeur.

The severe exterior of the house did not prepare one for the sumptuousness of the interior. I hardly know where to begin describing the wealth of gilt and paintings and ornaments. It was more like a museum or royal palace than a home. A butler who was knock-kneed and walked like a badger bowed us in. "Show the ladies a room, Petty, and tell cook we will have lunch for four in the morning parlor," our host said. "Lady Victoria will be joining us. Run upstairs and tidy yourself, Vickie."

We were shown to a charming chamber hung with Chinese paper, featuring ornate birds roosting in meager trees. The furnishings were clearly of the best quality: a canopied bed, a long carpet down the center of the room, and a scattering of mahogany tables and desks. "It looks as if he went to market and bought up everything in it," Mrs. Irvine said, staring all around.

"No, only the best."

I was never a guest in such a house before, but I had toured any mansion that was open to the public in the environs of Bath. I recognized quality, and I knew I was surrounded by it here. The change from my own spartan room at the seminary was so great as to overwhelm me. I had planned to set up a small, elegant apartment in London. I realized that my entire fortune would not furnish one room at Wycherly. The hand-painted paper on the walls would clean me out.

Dismayed, I went to the window. The view was magnificent. It showed a length of the serpentine water edged in rhododendrons. I tore myself away from it with reluctance. A maid came with water, and Mrs. Irvine and I made a hasty toilette, consisting mainly of removing our bonnets and pelisses and tidying our hair. While we worked I thought of the future. When I first came into my uncle's money, I entertained some secret hope that I was eligible to mingle with the very tip of the ton. This visit cured me of that notion. I would settle for my baronet, if I could find one to have me, but meanwhile I would enjoy seeing how the nobility disported itself.

I could not complain of noble manners today. Lord Marndale was awaiting us in his splendid entrance hall when we came downstairs, goggling all about us like a pair of bumpkins. Again I was struck by the eagerness of his manner. His eyes lit up and his lips lifted in a smile when we appeared. He placed a hand on my elbow and led us away from the abundance of gilt to a smaller parlor that was more livable. Sherry awaited us on a tray. Marndale poured. "This will keep us till lunch is served. Afterward I would like to show you around the park, or house if you prefer. The day is not so fine as it began," he mentioned, glancing out the window.

"There is no counting on the weather in April," Mrs. Irvine lamented. "I doubt if the *Prometheus* will set sail today as she was due to." She kept in touch with the wife of the captain who had replaced her husband aboard that ship.

"Will you be staying long at Wycherly?" I asked Lord Marndale to forestall a naval conversation. Once she gets started there is no holding her back.

"I hate being away in the spring, but I have business in London. I cannot stay here long. Of course, it's close enough that I can come home weekends. As soon as I find someone to tend Vickie, I shall get back to the House." His business was political business then, I deduced. My mind flew to Lydia Hopkins. "Would you know of a suitable lady, Miss Robsjohn?" he asked, as if reading my mind.

"I have a friend at the seminary at Bath who might be interested," I said. "A Miss Hopkins. She is accustomed to dealing with girls of Lady Victoria's age—well, a little younger, perhaps. She is a particular dab at French," I added, hoping to build Lydia up.

"It is really not the lessons I am so concerned about. Vickie is out of the schoolroom. It is rather a companion I have in mind. Victoria is . . . strongwilled," he said, choosing his word with care. "Well, you have met her. Do you think your Miss Hopkins could handle her?"

I dearly love Lydia. She is as close to a sister as I have ever had, but as I recalled Lady Victoria's stunt of the preceding night, I could not give an unqualified affirmative. If I was a trifle hard on the girls, Lydia was too soft. "Perhaps not Miss Hopkins," I said, my mind running over other teachers. Lydia would be wounded if I recommended anyone else over her head. And really the others were all old and stuffy.

"Think about it, and if you come up with a name, let me know before you leave."

We talked for ten minutes. Mostly Lord Marndale told us about the history of the house. It was amusing to hear the comments of Queen Elizabeth, a frequent visitor in the distant past, but my interest waned as he explained how some ancestor had built the place eons before and other ancestors had modified it here and there, removing statues and adding wings. I was not sorry when the butler summoned us to lunch.

Lady Victoria joined us. She continued polite if not exactly friendly. Soon the food and the selection of eating utensils required all my attention. I was not accustomed to such a plethora of cutlery to deal with. The array at either side of the plate seemed to go on forever. As course followed course, however, the use of each piece was discovered by keeping an eye on our host. We dined on fish and fowl, red meat and ragout and many vegetables, all of it delicious. It was too much of a good thing when fruit and cheese and a sweet followed.

"I can't find room for another crumb. I'll burst if I eat that cake, delicious as it looks," Mrs. Irvine said.

I felt the same, though I could not like her manner of expressing it. "Just coffee for me," I said.

As we drank our coffee Mrs. Irvine displeased me again. "We'd love to see all your finery, Lord Marndale, but Jennie and I really ought to be getting along if we hope to make London tonight," she said.

"Just a glimpse at the park," I told her. "I have been admiring that stream from my bedroom window, Lord Marndale."

"That is the work of Capability Brown," he said, and went on to tell us how the place had been a

36

field years ago, when his ancestor had lured Brown away from Blenheim Palace to oversee the doing of the park.

"We'll take a quick peek then," Mrs. Irvine agreed, none too happily.

We went directly from the table to the park. I admired the serpentine yet again. "There is so much more I would like to show you," Lord Marndale said. "Must you rush off?"

"We couldn't begin to see it all if we stayed a week," I said regretfully. Perhaps he was only repaying our kindness to his daughter, but if so, he did it with no air of conferring a favor. He was charming.

"You must have a look at *my* work at least. I have added a pavilion on top of a little mound in the west park. It is modeled after Brighton's Royal Pavilion, on a much less grandiose scale, of course. All I really mean is that it has a similar dome."

"Will it take long?" Mrs. Irvine demanded testily.

"Only a moment," he assured her, then led us on a ten-minute trek to see his new acquisition. It was not quite as large and grand as the prince's pavilion at Brighton but a more elaborate house than many people inhabit. Except, of course, that the walls were not enclosed from the waist up. This did not prevent him from having furnished the edifice. Lovely iron furniture, painted white, sat around the edges of the house. He had set a fast pace, and by the time we reached the pavilion Mrs. Irvine fell onto a chair, gasping. "I'm not as young as I was ten years ago," she panted, flapping a handkerchief to create a breeze.

Lord Marndale took me to the far side of the place to point out a view of three trees sitting in isolated splendor on a carpet of grass. "One always plants three. Two will not group," he explained. "As your companion is determined to drag you away so soon, I want to ask if you have thought of anyone who could look after Vickie."

You may deduce from the words that his interest was in finding a companion for his daughter. The delivery of them seemed to place the emphasis on Mrs. Irvine's cruelty in tearing me away. It was the way he said it, with his eyes lingering sadly on mine. It quite took my breath away.

"Perhaps Miss Hopkins would do," I said uncertainly.

"I would like someone like yourself. A lady of strong character and forceful personality. You certainly raked my hair with a stool at the Laughing Jack last night." He smiled a smile of unbounded approval.

"You were hiring adjoining rooms, and your daughter was not wearing a wedding ring," I pointed out. "What was one to think?"

"Why, I am very flattered, ma'am. I should have thought my advanced years must protect me from such unsavory suspicions."

This gave me an excuse to study him closely. Advanced years was certainly the wrong phrase. He was fully mature but still in the prime of life. "I don't see any silver in your hair yet."

"The words 'old enough to be her father' were bandied about, if I am not mistaken?" Lord Marndale's eyes had ceased meeting mine. They had lifted a few inches higher, to study my own hair. We had rushed out without bonnets.

"I expect my hair is ragged as a bird's nest," I said, lifting a hand to tidy it.

"You use the wrong simile. It is like a flame." His voice was soft, and when he lowered his eyes to meet mine I was extremely conscious of being a woman. "It is the way the sun strikes it from behind. A man could get singed from such hair as that."

I lifted my chin and replied lightly, "Not if he keeps his distance, sir."

He threw his head back and laughed. "Now that is the very sort of thing I admire in you, Miss Robsjohn. You brook no nonsense from anyone. Not even eligible gentlemen," he added enticingly. "You are quick-witted and clever. You even noticed Vickie wasn't wearing a wedding band. I require such a lady to stay with my daughter. Her last companion was not on to her curves. There was a man teaching her Italian . . ."

"Borsini," I nodded. "She mentioned him but assured me she had no intention of running away with him. Actually it was Mrs. Irvine who noticed the lack of a wedding ring."

"I don't suppose you could spare *her* to me?" he joked.

"She could not keep the pace. Only see how she is puffing."

"Don't you think it would be better to let her remain here overnight and recuperate?" he suggested. I just blinked in astonishment.

"We couldn't do that!"

"Is it your rigid schedule you are worried about or the proprieties? Surely the fact that you are accompanied by your chaperone makes it proper?"

"My rigid schedule is a myth," I smiled. Part of my smile was that he assumed my companion was a chaperone. A month ago I was the chaperone myself. Now I was young enough to require one.

"Then what is to prevent your remaining? The weather is by no means auspicious. You haven't seen half the house. I promise not to bore you with its history," he said, glinting a smile from his dark eyes. "I have kept a sharp eye on you, you see. I noticed what did not interest you. But there is a splendid library that might interest an ex-teacher, and a music room."

I trust his acuity did not penetrate all my tricks, for what interested me a deal more than stone and lumber was the owner of it all. "I don't know what Mrs. Irvine would say," I replied. But whatever she said, she would couch it in rustic terms that embarrassed me.

"Let us ask her."

He strode to her bench and we sat down beside her. "Have we tired you out completely?" he asked with an air of apology.

"I feel as if I've been ridden hard and put in the barn wet, but I can make it to the carriage."

His lips twitched in amusement. "Hard usage for a filly," he said.

"Filly? Ho, there is no need to sweet-talk me, Lord Marndale. It is Jennie who steers our ship. She is the one who decides where we heave to and when."

"We have been discussing your dropping anchor here for the night."

Her eyes flew to mine in alarm. "Isn't that wearing out our welcome?" she demanded. "All we did for Lady Victoria is rent her a truckle bed and stuff her with cream buns. There is no need to make us tenants for life, Lord Marndale."

"My intentions fall short of adoption," he assured her.

"What do you say, Jennie?" she asked.

"I think it would make a pleasant break in our journey." I could not repeat Marndale's fiction regarding worsening weather, as the sun came out from behind a passing cloud and blasted the pavilion in light.

"Well then, that's it. We'll stay. Odd that you, who in the usual way will argue with a gravestone, find no fault in interrupting our schedule," she added tartly. "If we are to stay, I'll go and have a lie down. I didn't get much sleep last night."

"Mea culpa," Lord Marndale murmured.

"What time should I be down for dinner?" she asked, hauling herself up from the bench.

"Sevenish?" Marndale said.

"We'll need our trunks unpacked if we are to muster in Bristol fashion."

Lord Marndale took her arm, and we all proceeded toward the house. "I hear the echo of the sea in your speech, I think?" he said.

"My husband was in the navy for twenty-five years. Davey Jones got him at Trafalgar. He was with Admiral Nelson."

"He died a hero's death. You must be proud of him."

"I'd rather a live husband than a dead hero, but that is neither here nor there."

"I have a cousin in the navy," he said, and chatted with her about nautical matters till we reached our destination.

I thought his intention was to entertain me himself, but when Mrs. Irvine went upstairs he said he had some business to tend to in his office and told me to make myself free of the house and grounds, which I did. The library was large enough to supply reading to a whole city, but I only glanced at a few shelves before going for an unguided tour of the house. It was unlikely I would ever be given carte blanche of such a place again, and I strolled at leisure through state rooms and art gallery, elaborate bedchambers, and later out to wander in the park and enjoy the terraced gardens. By late afternoon I was pleasantly fagged and returned to our room to speak to Mrs. Irvine and plan a toilette to match our surroundings.

Chapter Five

Mrs. Irvine was just rising from the bed and directed a penetrating eye on me. "He's up to something," was her opening salvo. "Have you figured out what it is?"

"Why, I expect he is just being polite."

"Pooh! I know when a man is trying to con me."

"You!"

"Yes, me as well as you. You must have noticed how long he talked to me about the navy and my husband. Hah, I am too old a cat to be fooled by a pup. He has something in mind, and I wish I knew what it was. When a lad bothers to pour the butter boat over the chaperone, he is to be watched by all hands."

"Surely you mean eyes."

"At sea it is the hands who stand watch. Our trunks are here. I sent your silk citron down to be pressed. It was a mass of wrinkles."

"Oh dear! I wanted to wear my bronze."

"That's a ball gown, Jennie! Don't make a cake of yourself. There is nothing so underbred as overdressing. He'll think you've never eaten dinner with a gentleman before."

"But his house is so fancy. And the citron washes my complexion out."

"Use my rouge pot," she said, and went to examine her own dark blue crepe. Like all her gowns it was plain, but she had a small strand of diamonds that would add to its dignity.

I had to make do with pearls, my one token of elegance, left me by my mother. My family belonged to the small landed gentry, with more breeding than capital. Papa was a younger son, and Mama's small fortune had been used to see the family through a few lean years when the farm was in difficulty. After Papa died, the mortgage ate up any money that was left. I could have gone to live with Papa's older brother, Seth, but I opted for independence.

I changed into the citron silk, an expensive error. I had seen something similar on a brunette with darker skin than mine, and it looked lovely. My pale complexion and Titian hair are better suited to stronger colors. We revealed our provincial origins by going downstairs at the appointed hour instead of being fashionably late. My chaperone's cosmopolitan doings were no help in that matter. "Nineteen hours is nineteen hours," she said, hustling me out the door at one minute to seven. No one else was about, and we sat in state alone in one of the drawing rooms, sipping a glass of sherry that Petty supplied us.

At ten past seven Lady Victoria and her father arrived, splendidly outfitted. She wore a charming ice blue gown. Her youth made her pearls eligible, but as I admired Lord Marndale's toilette I wished I had diamonds to complement the ruby in his cravat. Seeing that we were waiting, he did the gentlemanly thing and apologized for being late. He also complimented me on the citron silk, but it was to my flame of hair that his eyes returned more than once.

"We came down a moment early," I prevaricated. "Mrs. Irvine wished to see the gallery." I hoped the servants would not tell him we hadn't been near it.

"The Holbeins are considered the gems of the collection," he said. "I prefer the Italian style myself. What did you think of the Leonardo cartoons?"

Mrs. Irvine gave me a desperate look. "Lovely," she said, with an utterly transparent expression of incomprehension.

"I shall have Vickie painted when we go up to London. A pity Romney is dead. He did a lovely portrait of her mother," he added briefly, and talked a little about art.

I wondered where that Romney portrait was. I had not seen it in the gallery. In his bedroom, perhaps. I was curious to see it. His late wife must have been similar to Lady Victoria, as the daughter had not got her father's looks or coloring.

Soon dinner was announced, and we went in to a statelier meal than lunch, with a corresponding increase in china, crystal, and cutlery. The footmen hovering about the table unnerved me, but I tried to ignore them. Lord Marndale sensed our lack of ease and kept a lively flow of conversation going. When dinner was over he suggested Lady Victoria show me the library while he had his port.

She obeyed with apparent goodwill, but her help did not extend further than showing us to the room. She had no noticeable interest in the actual books but sat down with a magazine on one of the sofas scattered about the room and chatted to Mrs. Irvine while I studied the shelves. I kept an ear open and listened while I browsed. It always amazes me that Mrs. Irvine, with her shocking outspokenness, seldom makes an enemy.

"So you are not to get to Brighton after all, eh Lady Victoria?" Mrs. Irvine said.

"I don't mind so long as Papa is here. What I do not want is a horrid governess that he calls a companion."

"You wouldn't want to be left all alone!"

"Oh no, I should like to go to London with him."

"But it is so lovely here! What is missing that you could possibly want?"

"Young people. All Papa's friends are old, and he won't let me go to the local assemblies because of the sort of people who go there."

Public assemblies were my main entertainment in Bath. Mrs. Grambly provided a matron to accompany Lydia and myself to the Pump Rooms four times a year. She was no foe to marriage and liked to see her teachers make a match. How were young ladies to meet anyone if public assemblies were too déclassé?

"I expect you ride?" Mrs. Irvine prodded.

"Yes, but I don't like it much. I want to get a tilbury and learn to handle the ribbons. Can you drive, Miss Robsjohn?" she asked, turning to include me in the conversation.

How long it had been since I had the ribbons between my fingers! But one never totally forgets once the skill is mastered. "Oh yes," I said airily. "I am a fair fiddler."

Mrs. Irvine stared to hear it. I had got lost amongst the ancient Latin and Greek authors and asked Lady Victoria to lead me to the English novels. She seemed happy enough to oblige. We chatted about our favorite authors, while Mrs. Irvine leafed through the magazines. I was wrong to conclude the girl did not read. Lady Victoria liked Fanny Burney and Maria Edgeworth. My own preference was for Scott and the older writers—Fielding, Sterne.

After half an hour Lord Marndale joined us, and his daughter was packed off to bed with a dutiful exchange of pecks on the cheek. "How are you and Vickie getting along?" he asked. I took it for a banality, but he waited with apparent interest for my answer.

"Very well. We have been discussing our favorite authors."

"You will be appalled at her lack of taste."

"Burney and Edgeworth are well enough for light reading, so long as one is familiar with the more worthwhile writers as well," I said, with a touch of professional condescension.

"It is news to me that she reads anything thicker than a calling card. Though to be fair, I have seen her thumbing through an occasional chapbook or horrid gothic novel."

The tea tray was brought in, and I poured, feeling like the mistress of the place. One of my duties at the seminary was to instruct the ladies in the art of pouring tea. I knew to a nicety how to arch the wrist and how far to hold the spout above the cup. The conversation did not take the sort of turn I had anticipated. Lord Marnsdale subjected me to a severe quizzing on my career. Not the duration of it nor the reason I was teaching in the first place when I had some fortune but the actual subject matter and disciplinary measures.

"Did Mrs. Grambly permit the use of the strap?" he asked.

"No, she felt it proper for a boys' school but not for young ladies."

"How did she ride herd on the girls then?"

"We had occasionally to lock them in their rooms. For a serious infraction they might be deprived of an outing or a meal."

"You would be referring to doings with young gentlemen?"

Mrs. Irvine came to sharp attention. "Tell him about that hurly-burly chit who ran off with the dancing master."

"They were only gone for three hours in the middle of the afternoon," I reminded her.

"Ho, men can be up to as much mischief in daylight as in the dark, and it don't take three hours either."

"This one got up to no mischief, for I had seen him rolling his eyes at her the week before and took the precaution of discovering where he had rooms. Mrs. Grambly and I went after them and got the girl back with no harm done to her. We notified the other ladies' seminaries that the man was not to be trusted. It is the only way to deal with such creatures."

"That was well done of you, to have noticed their romance," he complimented.

"When you have young people in your trust you have to keep your wits about you," I said modestly.

"Had I known Mrs. Grambly's was so well staffed, I would have sent Vickie there," he said, with a bow that made it a personal compliment.

"She would have had experts in the various fields instead of expecting one woman to tutor her in everything," I pointed out.

"I fear I acted unwisely to keep her at home, but I wanted her near me. She could still do with some professional tutoring."

"Most girls leave school around her age. She would be the eldest girl there. I doubt she would be happy."

"Oh, it is out of the question now. She considers herself beyond the schoolroom. Have you thought of any friend or colleague who would be suitable to accompany her for the next year, till she is presented?"

"No, I cannot think of anyone at all. If it is only

a companion you want, surely you must know some gentlewoman who would welcome such a sinecure?" Poor relations existed in every family. As various aunts had been mentioned, I knew his extended family to be fairly large.

"I shall find someone, of course." He turned to include Mrs. Irvine in our conversation. "Are you ladies off to London for the Season?" She nodded.

"Not to make a formal debut," I said, "but only to absorb some culture—galleries, plays, concerts—and take in a few informal parties."

"That, too," my talkative friend said, "but since she has got her fortune, Jennie plans to nab a parti. We have a certain baronet in our eye. With ten thousand and some looks, she can aim that high, don't you think, Lord Marndale?"

The bluntness of her assertion left me pink all over. "I could really not care less whether I marry or not. It is the culture—"

"You're not old enough to have to settle for culture yet, Jennie. You have a few good years still in you."

Seeing my misery, Lord Marndale did the gentlemanly thing and changed the subject. "Mrs. Irvine mentioned a rigid schedule. I expect you have hired your house and servants?"

Nothing of the sort had been arranged. Our plan was to find a small apartment and hire a minimum of servants. "We shall do that after we arrive," I replied.

He looked surprised. "Ah. You might find some difficulty with the Season beginning."

Mrs. Irvine made another of her untimely eruptions into confidence. "If worse comes to worst, we can batten ourselves on Captain Smallbone, a friend of my late husband. He bought a small apartment house in Upper Grosvenor Square when he retired and ekes out his pension by renting a few rooms. I know he is not filled up, for I had a note from his wife just a week ago complaining that no one wanted the top floor because of the stairs. Jennie and I have strong limbs, however, and shan't mind an attic."

"Only as a last resort for a few days, till we can find something better," I added hastily.

"It will be cheap at least," Mrs. Irvine reminded me. "You'll find the interest on ten thousand does not go so far as it would in Bath. For myself, I would have settled for Mr. Fuller. Barring the squinty eye, he is not at all bad looking, and well to grass. He would have shut up his shop when he got your fortune."

"I assure you I have no intention of marrying a fifty-year-old draper!" I shot back angrily. "I am going to London—for the culture."

Lord Marndale considered all this a moment in silence, then said, "About London, would you not be wiser to write to an estate agent outlining your requirements and have him find you a place before you proceed to town?"

"What? Go all the way back to Bath?" Mrs. Irvine demanded, as though he were insane. I thought it a bizarre idea, too.

"No, no. I meant stay here. The fact is, till I can find a lady to tend Victoria, I am in something of a bind. You would be doing me a great favor to stay a week or two."

My first reaction was shock at the idea. My second was interest verging on delight. My third was dismay. Mrs. Irvine was right; he was up to something, and what I had to decide was whether it was a good thing for us. It would do us no harm to have spent a fortnight in a noble home. To arrive in London with an apartment already hired and waiting had its advantages. What mainly deterred me was plain impatience to reach the city. As I sat, mentally chewing over these conflicting factors, Lord Marndale continued talking.

I was not listening too closely, but it managed to get through to me that we might find ourselves putting up at a hotel in London for two weeks while waiting to find an apartment. That would obviously cost a fortune. He continued his persuasions.

"You will not want for company here. The neighbors are sociable and have not all left for London for the Season by any means. As to culture, the gallery has pictures, the library has books, and the stable can supply you with whatever mounts or carriages you require. My staff will look after all your needs as if you were family."

The more he talked, the better I liked it. "What would our duties be?" I asked.

"Why, just to bear Victoria company and see she does not get into mischief. If you can lead her to read an occasional book and see that she takes some exercise, it is all to the good. As I said, I must spend some time in London, but I shall be home as much as possible."

Better and better.

"While I am in London, I shall inquire of friends and relatives to see if I can find a suitable companion. I will be eternally in your debt if you oblige me in this manner."

This was best of all! Lord Marndale eternally in our debt. Peeling away the obvious hyperbole, it still suggested a continuing friendship. He could open any door for us in London.

"But why us?" I asked. "You don't even know us."

"You forget," he said with a dashing, confiding smile. "I have seen you under fire. I admire your spirit and your intelligence. You brooked no nonsense from me, and I am sure you would brook none from Vickie. You are accustomed to handling girls;

50

you are an educated, cultured lady who would serve as an excellent example to her."

"We could kidnap her and hold her to ransom for all you know," Mrs. Irvine pointed out.

He turned his charm in her direction. "I am not quite so negligent a father as that. Miss Robsjohn was recognized at the inn last night by a Mr. and Mrs. Shipley. Before you joined me in the parlor for breakfast, they informed me in no uncertain terms that I was traducing the character of a very superior lady. Had you not been defending yourself so superbly, they would have come to your defense. You taught their daughter at Bath. Emily was her name."

"The Shipleys! Did they see me in my disgrace!"

"No, they saw me in mine. Will you at least consider what I have asked? Sleep on it, and let me know in the morning."

His eagerness was writ large on his face. I looked a question at Mrs. Irvine. She shrugged, and I agreed to think about it. Actually, I could think of nothing else after we retired. This was not at all the way I had planned to begin my search for excitement and a husband, but it seemed an excellent way. After a few minor objections Mrs. Irvine was brought to appreciate at least the momentary advantages of the scheme.

When we went abovestairs we found our belongings had been moved to two sumptuous rooms, to prod us into acceptance by a greater show of richness. Our night things were laid out on the bed, and a cup of cocoa and a plate of biscuits awaited our pleasure. I doubted we would get such royal treatment at a hotel, and we certainly would not get it free of expense.

Chapter Six

In the morning I was up before the household and sat alone in the breakfast parlor. Even Mrs. Irvine was not up yet. Privacy was a rare privilege at the seminary. Any moment alone was treasured. Surveying my new position, I rather thought this would be my favorite part of the day, enjoying a quiet breakfast, surrounded by every sort of luxury. A month ago I was taking breakfast at a refectory table, facing a long row of giggling girls and a long day of riding herd on them.

I imagined I was mistress of all I surveyed, including the sun-dappled acres beyond the window. My appetite was still in its travelling mode, and I took a full meal from the covered dishes on the serving table. I was still eating when Lord Marndale came down.

When he stopped at the doorway and bowed his broad shoulders nearly filled the frame. He looked every inch the master of this fine home. What a fortunate man he was: wealthy, handsome, intelligent. The only misfortune that had ever befallen

52

him, so far as I knew, was losing his wife. His eyes wore an eager question.

"Good morning, sir. You may relax. I have decided to stay."

He bounded forward and placed an impetuous kiss on my forehead. "Thank God. And thank *you*, Jennie."

His enthusiasm left me warm with embarrassment. A nervous laugh escaped. "Jennie?" I exclaimed, hardly knowing what to say.

"I expect Miss Robsjohn will rap my knuckles for that familiarity, but as I have quite shamelessly used you as a friend, surely assuming the prerogative of using your name is only a minor infraction. I hope you will call me Marndale."

He took a plate and began filling it, still talking over his shoulder. "You found your new room with no trouble?"

"Bribery was not necessary, you know. The Chinese room was lovely."

"For a longer stay I thought you and your chaperone would like the privacy of separate rooms. Feel free to share the Chinese room if you prefer."

"No, I do like the privacy. I enjoyed being alone here, before you came. Not that I mean—"

He came to the table, a smile twinkling in his eyes. "My feelings are not so tender as that, Jennie." How odd it seemed to hear this mighty lord call me Jennie, as if we were old friends. "I did some thinking before I slept last night. Further fuel to entice you, in case you refused my request," he added with a playful grin. "I remembered I have a small apartment house on North Audley Street, just above Grosvenor Square."

"I would think it hard to forget such a possession!"

"I bought it this winter and have been having it redone. There are two apartments not taken yet. You can have one of them. It will be more convenient than your naval friend's place in Upper Grosvenor Square."

I feared that any possession of Marndale's must be beyond my purse and inquired for the rent. "Don't concern yourself about that. The use of it for the Season will be your repayment for helping me out with Vickie. If you wish to continue on after the Season, then we shall discuss terms."

"But I cannot take it without paying!"

He looked astonished. "None of my other tenants pay me. To tell the truth, I bought it as an investment for the future and find it an excellent storehouse for my various pensioners who would otherwise expect to stay here. Once you let them right into your home, you know, there is no turfing them out. I like my relatives, but I like them at a distance."

"I feel the same. My Uncle Seth wanted me to stay with him when Papa died, but I prefer him at arm's length." No more was said about the apartment. I didn't know whether I had accepted or not. I would have to discuss it with Mrs. Irvine.

"When did you lose your father?" he asked.

"Six years ago," I replied. He did not inquire if I had gone to work immediately, and I did not offer the information. We ate as we talked, with no feeling of constraint at all. Marndale was surprisingly easy to talk to till he came right out and said, "How long were you at Mrs. Grambly's?"

"Oh, a few years," I said vaguely, for I found it harder to tell an outright lie than I had thought I would.

"Was your father a naval man, like Mr. Irvine?"

"No, he had an estate in the country. Not a large one. He was a younger son."

"It is really none of my concern, but why did you choose to teach when it was not necessary—financially, I mean? Did you always harbor a wish to teach? Perhaps you are fond of youngsters?"

"Not in the least. I had very little money when Papa died. The mortgage, you know. My fortune—I

54

doubt you would call it that—only came to me last month, when a maternal uncle from India died."

"I would call ten thousand pounds or more a fortune. One can live with some of life's amenities on five hundred a year."

"Well then, it is a fortune—just barely."

"This baronet you have in your eye—"

"Good gracious, I am not hounding off to London after a husband! You must have noticed Mrs. Irvine has but one thing on her mind, but that is not to say I share her interest. If I happen to meet a gentleman I care for who also cares for me, I would consider an offer. If not, I shan't be desolated, I promise you."

He looked across the table with a lingering gaze. "I give you about three weeks before you're attached." It was my second blush that morning, and I swear I had not blushed in a decade. "Why are you not being presented formally?" he asked, pretending not to notice my rosy cheeks.

I had no intention of admitting I had no suitable connections. "Everything happened so suddenly, there was not time to arrange it. I just decided to go along to London and enjoy a little culture, as I said. I have lived near or in Bath all my life. I intend to return there eventually."

He cocked his head to one side and studied me. "Bath is for valetudinarians. You must be strikingly out of place."

"I have many friends in Bath."

He continued studying me. "What a slow bunch of tops they must be to have let you escape."

I laughed. "I took my money and ran. There was no stampede to attach me when I was a working lady."

"Not even from Mr. Fuller?" I was amazed that he recalled the draper's name.

"Surely more than one man is necessary to form a stampede."

It was at this moment, almost verging on intimacy, that Lady Victoria joined us. She looked sharply from me to her father. "Enjoying a new flirtation, Papa?" she sniffed, and placed a cool peck on his cheek.

"You must mind your manners, miss," he said jovially. "You do not want to give Miss Robsjohn a disgust of you or she will change her mind about staying with us."

She turned a piercing and very mature gaze on me. "Oh, you have agreed to stay. How lovely." But her flashing blue eyes belied the words. Then she turned to her father. "You *did* tell Miss Robsjohn that I am no longer in the schoolroom, Papa? She is staying as a companion, not a governess."

"She is in loco parentis, and will inform me of any misconduct. But we must not frighten her." He turned to me. "Vickie's problem is ennui. She is a restless girl. Keep her occupied, and she will give you no trouble."

"When are you leaving, Papa?" she asked.

"As soon as I've finished breakfast. I expect to be home Friday afternoon. Can you two ladies amuse yourselves while I'm gone?"

"I trust we can," I told him, with a leery glance at Lady Victoria. She went to the serving table and began filling her plate.

Lord Marndale hastily finished his breakfast, kissed his daughter good-bye, shook my hand, asked me to convey his adieux to Mrs. Irvine, and left. I regretted that Lady Victoria had joined us, as her staring presence prevented any warmer farewell.

"What do you suggest we do today, Lady Victoria?" I asked in a friendly way.

"I am going into the village," she replied, with another of those ice cold looks.

"Excellent. What village is that?"

"Chiddingfold, of course."

That "of course" revealed her mood. If she

thought to intimidate me with poor manners, she was much mistaken. "I look forward to it."

"Oh, do you want to come along?"

"That is what 'I look forward to it' usually means."

Her lips clenched, but she dared not be too rude. "I shall be leaving as soon as I finish eating."

"I'm afraid you must wait till Mrs. Irvine is down, to see if she wishes to go with us. Naturally you will not want to offend your father's guest by leaving her out."

"Guest? Is Papa not paying you?" she asked boldly.

"No, he isn't. As you were at such pains to point out I am a companion, not a governess, I thought you realized it."

"Hired companions are usually paid, too."

"Hired companions are always paid. It is implicit in the phrase, but I am *not* a *hired* companion."

She attacked her meal. I sat without trying to nudge her into conversation. The chit had the manners of a guttersnipe the minute her father was away. I had dealt with many such an unruly noble brat in the past. Ingratiation was not the way to subdue them. Their ill manners must be met with firm control. I stared while she ate. She handled her cutlery like a lady but ate with more haste than was seemly. I let her see by the sneer on my lips that I was appalled at her manners.

"There is no need to gobble your food," I said cooly. "Mrs. Irvine has not even come down yet."

Bereft of a setdown the child said, "Then you will have time to change your gown, Miss Robsjohn. Or did you actually mean to go into the village in that gown?"

I wore a perfectly respectable sarsenet gown, plain but well cut. "No, I thought I might wear my tiara and diamonds."

"I didn't know schoolmistresses had tiaras."

"There is obviously a good deal you do not know."

"At least I know why you are here," she flashed back.

57

"I should hope so. Your father made it perfectly clear, I think."

"You hope to get an offer from him, but you are wasting your time, Miss Robsjohn. He *never* offers for my governesses."

I found a smile more likely to infuriate her than a hot objection, and smiled. She rose with half her breakfast still on her plate and said, "I shall be in my room. Pray have me called when Mrs. Irvine is ready to leave."

"You may speak to Petty on your way up."

Her lips drew into a thin line that destroyed her looks, but she did not answer back. She left without saying more. I understood now why she had taken me in such violent dislike. She was afraid she might be saddled with me as a stepmama. I could hardly blame her, but still her atrocious manners must be brought under control.

Mrs. Irvine soon came down and heard the story while she ate. "I'll just ignore her and act as though nothing is wrong," she decided. There is a solid bulwark of common sense beneath Mrs. Irvine's rough exterior.

"That will be best. Ah, here she is now!"

She appeared at the doorway already in her bonnet and pelisse, both the very latest word in fashion. "What a lovely bonnet, Lady Victoria," Mrs. Irvine exclaimed with a smile.

This greeting met with the young lady's approval. She had apparently decided to take Mrs. Irvine on as an ally, for she spoke to her in a friendly way about the bonnet while pointedly ignoring me. She told Mrs. Irvine the milliner in Chillingfold came from France and made a very decent bonnet.

It was Lord Marndale's chaise that awaited us at the front door. Not the travelling carriage of yesterday but a lighter one, harnessed up with a team of grays. The day was fine, and the village only a few miles away. Barring a little constraint within the vehicle, the trip was pleasant, as was Chillingfold. A church with a lancet window was one of the prominent features of architecture in the village. Across from it was the village green, complete with duck pond. There were benches, and some ladies strolling about, showing off their new spring finery. The driver took the carriage to the inn and we alit. The Crown Inn, a drapery shop, a milliner, a cobbler, and a few other shops made up the core of the town with houses spreading beyond.

"What is your errand here?" I asked Lady Victoria.

"I need some embroidery threads," she said, and headed across the street to the drapery shop. She deigned to tell Mrs. Irvine that she was making her papa a pair of embroidered slippers for his birthday. I bought a quite useless length of blue ribbon, and Mrs. Irvine succumbed to a pair of silk stockings. This done, we returned to the street.

The church was the next stop. The windows were odd, of stained glass but made up of little fragments. Lady Victoria explained that in medieval days the town was a glass-making center. From there we joined the other idlers on the village green. Before we had made half a tour we were joined by some friends of Lady Victoria's.

A rough-and-tumble set of young ladies came running forward. Beneath their overly ornate bonnets wisps of dull blond curls peeped out. Their faces had the coarse-featured look and sallow complexions of the underbred. "Vickie! You're back! How lovely. Desmond has gone into a decline worrying about you. Can you come home for lunch, or is your papa with you?"

I came to attention at these remarks. So there was a young man involved! And one that Marndale did not approve of. I doubted he would approve of these hoydens either. Though nominally ladies, they were extremely unfinished articles. I knew now why Lady Victoria had resisted my company. She wanted to consort with this pair of trollops and possibly meet Desmond. Her flaming cheeks were as good as an admission.

"Miss Robsjohn, Mrs. Irvine, I would like you to meet Miss Simon and her sister, Miss Bea," Lady Victoria said. "They live near us, in that big red brick house we passed on the way into the village." I remembered a substantial house but was curious to know more of their background.

"We come from London," Miss Simon assured me.

Their papa, I assumed, had made his fortune in trade and retired to the country to become genteel.

"We are from Bath," I replied, including Mrs. Irvine with a gesture.

"Oh lud! Poor you!" Miss Simon exclaimed. "Mama dragged us there last year for a holiday. I would as lief holiday in Coventry. It is dull as ditch water. More Bath chairs than curricles, and the gents all stiff as starch. They wouldn't look at you twice if you danced a jig in church. And are you Vickie's new governess?"

"Just friends," I replied grandly.

"Is your papa home?" Miss Bea asked Lady Victoria.

"No, he is in London."

The eyes of the Simon sisters turned to examine me. "Can you come home for a cup of tea at least?" Miss Bea asked Lady Victoria.

"Someone will be mighty hurt if you don't," Miss Simon tittered.

Lady Victoria did not even bother asking my permission for the visit. "I'm afraid not today. We have to be getting home."

"Tomorrow then? Come for tea." It was Miss Bea who urged this scheme. "We'll be expecting you. Now don't let us down."

"I'm afraid it's too early to make a commitment.

So nice to have met you." I put a hand on my charge's elbow and led her away. The mutinous eye she turned on me clearly expected some outpouring of condemnation, but I refused to oblige her.

I said only, "How encroaching those girls are. One would think they owned you to hear them order you about. Incredible!" After that I ignored the incident as if it had never happened. We left the green very soon, and as we went for the carriage I said, "It is such a fine day, we should give you a driving lesson this afternoon, Lady Victoria. Does your father have anything suitable?"

A smile of surprise greeted this suggestion. "His curricle is at home. He won't want us to use his grays, but we can use the older pair of bays. He took his better team to London."

"Do you think he would object to my teaching you?"

"Oh, no! He has been promising to teach me himself forever, but he is so busy, you know. Are you a good fiddler, Miss Robsjohn?"

"I was fair to middling in my day. It will take me an hour to refresh my skills."

"We'll have lunch early. Papa says the best road for me to learn on would be the road to Willigan's farm. There is very little traffic there except for an occasional haywain or dung cart or old Ned Willigan's jig."

The trip home was livelier and better-natured than the trip to the village, despite her loss of meeting with Desmond. I decided it was sheer boredom that led her into such unsuitable companions as the Simons. I must keep her occupied, and we would get on fine.

Chapter Seven

Marndale's sporting carriage and second-best team of bays awaited us at the front door after lunch. His second-best team were still a friskier-looking pair than I had ever driven before. Their coats gleamed like polished mahogany in the sunlight, highlighting the swell of powerful chests and lean, long legs. With my heart pulsing in my throat, I went out to try my skill with them. If I failed, I would lose the vestige of respect I had gained from Lady Victoria. Mrs. Irvine came to the door to see us off with the plan of spending a quiet afternoon looking over the house after we left.

Though powerful and full of life, the pair were sweet goers with silk mouths. They responded to the lightest touch. I knew before I reached the main road that I had not lost my skill. How exhilarating it was to canter along with the sun beating on my shoulders and a smoothly-moving rig beneath me. I began figuring what corners I would have to cut to buy such a carriage for myself. It could only be done if I omitted the London holiday. There was a moment of panic when a coach and four were spotted in the distance galloping toward us at breakneck speed. As they drew nearer the coach got wider and wider till I feared I would have to go in the ditch to avoid a crash. But I pulled as far as I could to my side, the coach driver pulled to his, and we squeaked past without incident.

"Well done, Miss Robsjohn!" Lady Victoria exclaimed. "Just like Lettie Lade."

"Who is Lettie Lade?"

"Haven't you heard of her? She is all the crack in London. Sir John Lade's wife—she is a famous whip, though not very good ton, Papa says. Too fast by half." I saw I could learn a few things from Lady Victoria if I kept my ears open. I was entirely ignorant of the social *on dits* of London. "When can I try?" she asked soon.

"As soon as we reach Willigan's road. Where do I turn off?"

"Just at that big elm tree by the corner. Turn right."

The turn was executed without incident. I had managed two miles without disgracing myself, but my arms were fatigued from tension, and I was happy to turn the reins over to my charge. I showed her the proper way to arrange the leathers between her fingers to allow free and equal pressure on all reins.

"They are easy goers. Don't yank on the reins to stop them but just pull gently."

"Papa already told me that much. Giddap." She gave them their head, and we were off at a stately trot.

Being young and full of confidence she was eager to see them canter, but I held her down to a trot on the first lesson. For an hour we drove up and down Willigan's road. The lesson was enlivened by a meeting with two jigs and a farm cart, both of which she passed successfully.

"Can't I let them canter, just the last mile?" she begged as we neared the end of the road.

"Very well, but pull in at the corner and let me drive home. The main road is too busy, but you'll be driving it within the week. You have a natural talent." She beamed with pleasure.

The canter was beyond her. The nags got out of rhythm, and we finished the lesson at an uneven, jiggling gait. I thought it a good lesson to us both. She must not have more confidence than skill, and I must not let her talk me into folly. I intimated the former in my schoolmistressy way.

"Oh, Jennie!" she laughed. "Don't turn into a governess on me again."

I was surprised at her calling me Jennie but pleased at her unconsciously friendly speech. "I heard Papa call you Jennie," she said, with a curious light in her eye. "Do you mind my doing so, as you are a friend, not a governess?"

I was happy to be free of anything that smacked of the schoolroom and gave her permission. We got on better after the lesson. That evening Victoria (she asked me to call her so) and Mrs. Irvine and myself retired to a small, cosy saloon to chat while Victoria worked on her father's slippers and I mended a rip under the arm of a favorite blouse.

"If it's worn out, why don't you throw it away?" she asked innocently.

"It is not worn out. A seam has split, that's all. One does not discard perfectly good clothing.'

"It doesn't look new. The nap is all worn off."

"I've had it two years." She laughed. "You don't realize what a privileged position you hold, Victoria. Most young ladies have to count their pennies. It cost me a whole day's work to buy the material

64

for this blouse and three evenings' labor to make it."

"Did you make it yourself?" she asked, eyes wide. This was what impressed her and not the cost.

"Certainly I did. I did all my own sewing till I inherited a little money from an uncle."

"You are so capable, Jennie," she said, shaking her head in wonder. "I wish I could be like that."

"What is to prevent it? You're able-bodied and intelligent."

"That is a very nice stitch you are setting there in your papa's slippers," Mrs. Irvine pointed out.

"And soon you'll be driving well, too," I added.

"Yes," she said doubtfully, "but you are *really* independent. Papa has always taken care of me. You take care of yourself completely. You do your own hair. You don't have a dresser or anything."

"My circumstances were different from yours. We must each learn the duties we have to perform in life. For you that will be running a gentleman's house. What you ought to do is spend some time with the housekeeper learning such things. I would be no help to you there. I would be happy, however, to accompany you in your charitable work while I am here."

Her face was a perfect blank. "What charitable work?"

"Why, visiting your father's tenants and the sick of the parish, helping out at the church, and the local orphanage . . ." I continued with a list of the usual good deeds of a lady, but none of the items elicited any understanding.

She read the disapproval on my brow, and said, "I have been in the schoolroom till now."

"Now that you are out of it you will want to assume the duties of a lady. One cannot be expected to be treated as an adult if she behaves like a child, can she? You must bear in mind that privileges im-

65

pose an obligation, Victoria. How many girls do you think live in such a home as this, surrounded by every luxury? My room at the seminary was not much bigger than the clothes press in my room here, and I was not amongst the truly unfortunate. From my tiny stipend, earned by the sweat of my brow, I always designated a tithe for charity."

She was aghast at this plain speaking. "No one ever told me! They have been treating me like a child!"

"Someone has dropped you the hint now. We shall see if you are mature enough to act on it."

"I have dozens of gowns I should be happy to be rid of."

"Silken gowns would not be much good to the poor, who do strenuous labor for a living. One cannot pick stones for the road or work in a dairy in a silk gown. Giving what you no longer want is not true charity, Victoria. You must give what will be useful—which is not to say you cannot give those excess gowns to some relative less favored than yourself."

"I'll do it tomorrow. And we shall visit Mrs. Munson, too. She had twins last week, Jennie. Would you not like to see them?"

"Indeed I would. Who is this Mrs. Munson?"

"She is a tenant."

"I daresay she would appreciate a meal from your kitchen—soup or a joint or something of that sort—while she is unable to cook."

A pensive look settled on her pretty little face. "I wonder how the family eat while she is in bed. They have no servants."

I was happy to see I had directed her thoughts in the proper direction and encouraged her along these lines. It was arranged that our driving lesson the next day would take us to Mrs. Munson's house, bearing food.

Lady Victoria took her new duties seriously. A hamper large enough to feed an army was delivered to the Munsons' house the next day. The twins were delightful—boys with golden wisps of curls and faces like angels and tiny little fists. The mother looked more shocked than pleased to see us but thanked us very prettily. Victoria was allowed to hold one boy, I the other. The strength of the emotion that seized me as I held the infant was astonishing. I felt a fierce love of it. How much stronger must the sensation be when a lady holds her own child in her arms?

I began to feel, over the few days before Marndale's return, that Victoria had been a bud waiting to open. A little guidance was like sun and water to her better nature. Her hankering for my approval was almost pathetic. She would come running to me, telling me she was cutting flowers for the church altar, or sending some clothes to someone called Cousin Alicia, who apparently felt the lack of new gowns; and once she said she had set aside a tenth of her allowance to give the vicar to dispense to worthy parishioners.

"That was well done, Victoria. Don't you feel the better for it?" I asked.

"Oh, yes, I never felt so happy in my life." She did look more alive. Her eyes glowed, and her face had entirely lost its sullen look. "There is a great pleasure in doing good deeds. I am thinking of devoting my life to charity."

I felt sure this white hot enthusiasm would dwindle to a more acceptable level with no urging from me, but the seed had been planted, and she would, hopefully, do as much as she ought.

We were now close enough that I ventured to quiz her about the Simon family. "Who is this Desmond the girls mentioned?" I asked calmly.

"He's their older brother."

"Handsome, is he?"

"He was sent to a good public school and has better manners, though he is not precisely handsome."

"Is he a beau?" I asked quizzingly.

"Oh, no, I am just using him for practice when I make my curtsey next year."

"That is rather cruel to Desmond, is it not? You might raise hopes that you have no plan to fulfill."

"I never thought of that! I am so selfish!"

"A lady always treats others as she would wish to be treated if she were in their place. Now you would not want Desmond toying with your emotions, would you?"

"No, toying and playing are for children. I shall be a little cooler in future. Still friendly, for I must not hurt their feelings, but cooler. Perhaps you and I shall drop in one day," she said, for all the world like a dowager arranging her strategy. "But I shan't flirt with Desmond."

Marndale was to return on Friday afternoon. Victoria was eager to be home to greet him and looking her best. "For he does not usually come alone," she mentioned with a teasing look. "You must tidy your hair, Jennie, and wear your nicest gown. Perhaps some of his guests will be bachelors."

There was a place for building character and doing good deeds but that need not prevent a lady from making a push to attach a husband. I did as she advised and was sitting with Victoria in state in the garden with a dainty umbrella to protect our complexions when the carriages rumbled up the drive.

"Only one extra carriage," Victoria said, peering through the privet hedge. "I wonder who it can be. There is a crest on the door. Let us go out and meet them."

With Victoria for an excuse I did exactly what I had been wanting to do myself. Who should step down from the other carriage but Lord Anselm, brother to Lady Mary Anselm, an ex-pupil. I recognized his long, lean frame and curly head four yards away, and he recognized me as well.

"Miss Robsjohn, what the deuce are you doing here?" he smiled, and came pouncing forward to shake my hand like an old friend. I had forgotten his chin was so huge. It hung like a beard made of flesh.

"I am keeping Lady Victoria company while her father looks about for a permanent companion." I noticed from the corner of my eye that Marndale was looking at me, waiting for me to welcome him; but I could not cut Lord Anselm off too abruptly.

"I had no notion you were connected to Marndale," he continued, "though I realized, of course, you were dashed out of place in that school in Bath." I flushed with pleasure and admitted I was not connected to Marndale. "Charles, you sly dog," he continued, turning to Marndale, "you did not tell me you knew Miss Robsjohn. I should have known when you mentioned your guest's fiery crown." His eyes slid toward my curls in a knowing grin.

I derived considerable amusement from Marndale's shocked face. It amused me, too, that he had been giving his guest a description of me. I went forward to shake his hand and make him welcome at his own home.

"Jennie, how has everything been going?"

"Victoria and I have managed to fill our days most agreeably."

"Jennie has reformed me, Papa!" Victoria laughed.

A flash of interest lit his eyes at our easy rapport and use of first names. "I recognized Jennie as an extremely capable lady from the start, but I had no notion she was a miracle worker."

"Oh, Papa, surely I was not that bad! Just selfish and spoiled."

They began walking toward the door together, and I fell into step behind with Lord Anselm. Our conversation was about what was to be expected. He asked when I had left the school, and why, and paid a few compliments to the effect that I must be sorely missed there. His business with Marndale was political. He had come for the weekend to iron out the details of some bill for presentation in Parliament. I made sure to mention I would soon be in London, and he asked for permission to call without blinking an eye. My being at Wycherly put me on a completely different social level, as I had suspected it would.

We all went into the saloon, and Mrs. Irvine came to join us. I have given her short shrift in my account. She did not accompany Victoria and myself on our outings. There was plenty to entertain her in the house and gardens. She liked to sit at a window with a good view, doing her netting. She took many strolls through the park for exercise and struck up a friendship with the housekeeper and the gardener; and, of course, spent time with myself and Victoria as well.

Lord Anselm took up the chair beside me and continued his overtures at friendship while we had our sherry and biscuits. "Fancy Mary not telling me you had left the seminary. Of course, I have not heard from her in a month, but she might have written me the news. You were her favorite teacher, Miss Robsjohn. Her letters were always full of your doings. She is due home herself in the summer for a year's ripening in the country before I trot her off to the Season. She gave me a detailed account of the nature hikes you took the girls on last year. Once you remained outdoors overnight, I believe?"

"Yes, it was our intention to live off the land for

two days—with a little help from a picnic basket and two footmen to build fires and so on. The headmistress had been reading Mrs. Brunton's *Self-Control*, and was greatly impressed with the heroine's ingenuity in the face of hardship. It was the girl's escaping her attacker in America by floating downstream in a birchbark canoe that particularly impressed her. Rafting was a feature of our great outing."

"You and I should try camping in the wilderness overnight, Jennie," Victoria said. I did not realize till she spoke that both she and her father were listening to Anselm and me. She continued talking to her father. "Jennie is making me self-reliant, too, Papa. She is teaching me to drive, and we have been visiting the poor and Mrs. Munson. The twins are beautiful. Oh, and we are taking flowers to the church tomorrow so they will be fresh for the Sunday service."

"All this in three days!" Marndale asked, laughing, but there was approval in his manner. "I have always heard a leopard does not change its spots."

"Ho, they would wear stripes or plaid or a monkey suit if Miss Robsjohn told them to," Anselm said.

"Good gracious! You all make me sound like a tyrant. I hope I am not so bad as that. Can you not come to my aid, Mrs. Irvine?"

"You are looking so pleased with all the attention that I didn't want to spoil your moment of glory. It's not often you have two gentlemen hanging on your every word."

"And one lady," Victoria said, laughing at my blush.

"Aye, for *this* one isn't interested," Mrs. Irvine said, with a sour look.

"How have you been getting along, Mrs. Irvine?" Marndale inquired, as being ignored had put her out of frame.

"This is Jennie's canard. I'll let her milk it. I have been taking it easy and letting her do all the

71

work. I am like a blister. I only show up after the work is done."

"What work?" I asked, pleased at all the attention. "It is Victoria who has been doing all the good works. I have done nothing but talk."

"You were always good at that," Mrs. Irvine slid in.

"I have been lecturing the hoyden for sixteen years," Marndale objected. "You must be an extremely efficacious talker, Jennie."

"She could talk the hide off a cow," Mrs. Irvine informed him.

"By Jove, I like a lady who has some conversation," Anselm said. "Trying to get a word out of most ladies is as futile as shearing a pig. Nothing comes of it. When may I expect to see you in London, Miss Robsjohn?" he asked eagerly.

"The week after next."

Marndale's head slewed sharply toward us. I intercepted a look and asked if he had had any luck in finding a companion for Victoria.

"Truth to tell, Anselm and I have been so busy with government matters that I had time to do no more than put out a few feelers. I've also inserted an advertisement in the journals. I hope by next week I may find someone."

"If it will mean hastening Miss Robsjohn to London, I shall give you a hand," Anselm said. "I know it is the very devil to find a good companion. There aren't many as capable as Miss Robsjohn around." He drew his chair a little closer and began to talk about Mary.

His friendliness was pleasing, but I regretted that he should monopolize me. The meeting soon broke up. The gentlemen wanted to bathe after their trip, and we ladies had to make a grand toilette for dinner.

Chapter Eight

Having Marndale home and a guest besides made dinner special. I wanted to wear my bronze, but again Mrs. Irvine deterred me. "Best save your fine feathers, Jennie. What will you wear to stun Marndale if he has a real party while we're here?" she asked in her commonsensical way. I wore the citron complexion destroyer again. Anselm praised it to the skies.

"We did not see this side of Miss Robsjohn at the seminary!" he exclaimed after three or four outrageous compliments. I wished he would not harp on the seminary, but he was so complimentary that it is mere carping to mention it.

"I doubt you heard the rough side of her tongue either, as I have done," Marndale said, and went on to describe our intitial encounters with many jokes and much laughter.

"No, surely he did not accuse you of being an abbess!" Anselm expostulated. "It's like calling a judge a felon. Unthinkable!"

"She called me a rake!" Marndale defended.

"Ah, but that is not *entirely* unthinkable, is it, Charles?" Anselm laughed.

Marndale gave an uneasy look and sought refuge in French. *"Honi soit qui mal y pense."*

I called them to account. "Gentlemen, a little decorum if you please. Small pitchers have large ears." I glanced at Victoria.

"You're the one who brought up the abbess business," Mrs. Irvine reminded me. So helpful of her!

I may be blowing my own horn to say it, but there was a feeling in the air that the two gentlemen were in competition for my favors that evening. As surely as Lord Anselm recalled some incident from the seminary (where else?), Marndale would retaliate with an account of some more recent occurrence. After dinner and after the gentlemen had taken their port, they joined us in the saloon and we discussed how to pass the evening. As there was only Anselm from outside, Lady Victoria was allowed to stay up with the adults. Really she seemed more mature already.

"Shall we take the ladies for a ride to Reigate tomorrow?" Marndale asked with the air of conferring a treat. "A little shopping, luncheon at an inn . . ."

"I shall be busy, Papa," his daughter replied, very high on her dignity. "I have promised Vicar flowers for the church, and I will be taking Mrs. Munson a basket while she is not feeling quite the thing, you know. Then I must have my driving lesson."

She chose a poor time to insist on her new regime in my view. I would have enjoyed the outing to Reigate, but I could not like to deter her when it was all my own idea.

"Our calendar is full, Marndale," I joked. "You must make an appointment in advance if you wish to entertain your daughter."

"Then I shall ask you all to leave next weekend open. I will be bringing a few guests home. We'll have a dinner party and perhaps some informal dancing."

My mind flew to my bronze, happy that Mrs. Irvine had not let me wear it before.

"We must have our overnight camping expedition before the weekend, Jennie," Victoria said. It seemed quite a settled thing in her mind. She was determined to do anything my other girls had done. "Perhaps you could suggest a safe spot for the venture, Papa?"

"I don't know that I approve of the venture at all," he said doubtfully.

"Fear not, Marndale," Anselm told him. "With Miss Robsjohn at the helm, nothing would dare go amiss. The very birds in the trees and deer in the forest rush to do her bidding."

"But do the winds and rain?" Marndale asked, with a quizzing smile in my direction. That look suggested that they did. He accepted the plan with a joke and discussed a likely location with Victoria. I was not familiar with the territory, but she knew the area he referred to. He mentioned wooded acres with some pond or river or lake for us to take a raft out on after we had constructed it.

Then he turned to speak to me. "You will take a few servants along, I trust? The Hubbards are a good, reliable pair and young enough to enjoy this unusual outing. He works in my stable but would prefer to live in a tree or a hollow log. He goes into the forest as often as his duties permit. Mrs. Hubbard helps out in the kitchen and can help you with the cooking. Be sure you take plenty of warm blankets. I'll speak to Hubbard myself and see that he is aware of your needs."

"I am not a child, Papa!" Victoria objected. "You may leave the arrangements to Jennie and me."

He just shook his head in wonderment. The evening passed swiftly with no special entertainment. We all agreed that cards were a dead bore and settled instead on various childish word games, which involved many wretched jokes and worse puns. Before retiring I had a moment with Marndale to discuss Victoria's transformation.

"It is almost incredible, the change in her. She is not only in a better mood, she actually looks better," he said.

"It is being out in the fresh air that accounts for it."

"Have the Simon girls been to call?" he asked with an air of diffidence.

"No, nor has she been there to meet Desmond. I assume that is what really bothers you?"

"There is nothing particularly amiss with the family, but I would not like her to become intimate with them. It was Miss Clancy who instituted the friendship. She had her eye on Desmond, I expect."

"And Desmond had his on Victoria. I thought Miss Clancy got married recently? Why would she be dangling after Simon?"

He hesitated a moment before replying. "To make her beau jealous, perhaps," he said. I felt the name Anselm float in the air between us. There was something in the way he studied me, with a curiously pensive expression. "There is nothing like competition to waken a man up."

My duty was to fail to read anything personal in this speech. "We met the girls in the village the day you left. I believe I have talked Victoria out of intimacy."

"How did you manage that, Jennie?"

"Why, I told her it would be unkind of her to lead Desmond on if she had no intention of having him." When I saw the mischief inherent in my words, I

76

hastened on. "But really it is the driving lessons that distract her."

"That was well done of you to teach her. How is she doing?"

"Remarkably well."

"I fancy she has an excellent instructor in the formidable Miss Robsjohn." This speech was accompanied by a small bow. "Is there anything you cannot do?"

"Yes. I have very little notion how to run a household. Our housekeeper did that when Papa was alive, and I went from home to the seminary. Your housekeeper should give Victoria some instructions." I had just let slip I'd been teaching six years. Marndale did not look surprised.

"Vickie was never interested before, but since her change of heart no doubt she will give it a try. I scarcely recognize her since I returned. The change, I need hardly say, is all for the better. How did you manage the miracle, Jennie?"

"I appealed to her finer instincts. I tried to make her aware of her privileged position. Noblesse oblige and all that."

He grinned. "I hadn't thought of trying guilt."

"Perhaps you were not so aware of her privileges, as you share them."

He rewarded my impudence with a wry smile. "Very likely. But I hope you will not chastise me for failing to shoulder my responsibilities. I have been working like a slave these past days and shall burn the midnight oil with Anselm tonight while you rest. You and Anselm are old friends, I take it? Were you neighbors before your father died?"

"Oh no. I only met him at the seminary, where Lady Mary was a student."

His eyes widened at that. "One cannot blame *him* for being a slow top. The relationship seemed . . . warmer than a merely professional one."

77

"We met several times over the years. We are hardly bosom bows."

"Good," he said softly, while a small smile played over his lips. Then he bowed, wished me good night, and returned to his office.

I pondered that quiet "good" while I undressed. There was nothing amiss with Anselm's character. Such things become known at the seminary, and in any case Marndale would not have brought a scoundrel into his own house. So what could he mean? I could not think of any plausible reason for the remark, but the implausible one pleased me greatly.

That weekend passed in a delightful blur of activity. By rushing all Victoria's good works and her driving lesson into the morning we found time for a drive with the gentlemen in the afternoon. Not to Reigate but along a country road where a riot of wild flowers spangled the meadows and perfumed the air. We got out and took a leisurely stroll. Anselm was attentive. Marndale was unhappy with the attentions, and Lady Victoria watched the show with the curious face of a dowager, not disapproving exactly but not entirely happy either. It was for Mrs. Irvine, who sat bobbin during the trip, to call me to account after we returned home and I was boasting a little of my conquests.

"You were about as subtle as a bull in rut, Jennie," she cautioned. "You made a cake of yourself, hanging on to Lord Anselm's arm and laughing your head off at every foolish word he uttered. Only lightskirts are so eager to please men. Marndale is not a fool. He could see you were angling for the man."

"But did you see how it annoyed him?" I riposted.

"Yes, very likely he wants you to take on his

daughter till she marries and nabbing Lord Anselm would interfere with that. I admit you have done good work there but don't go imagining there is anything personal in his interest."

Her plain speaking quite took the wind out of my sails. This perfectly logical idea had not occurred to me, but as I reviewed our various conversations I had to admit his kind words centered almost totally on my way with Victoria. Even that quiet "good" that had kept me awake last night took on a less attractive hue.

"Anselm didn't seem to mind. He would be a pretty good catch, don't you think?" I said offhandedly, for I would not satisfy her to let her know I was cross.

"He's so ugly he shouldn't be allowed out in daylight without a bag over his head."

"Ugly! Just because his hair is a little frizzy . . ."

"A little frizzy? He looks like a Hottentot! And it was his *chin* I was referring to. If it were any longer, he'd need a wheelbarrow to keep it off the floor."

"What nonsense. All the girls at the seminary called him handsome."

"Aye, they'd call a 'rangutang handsome if he had a handle to his name. And never mind avoiding the issue. Did Marndale ask you to remain on longer? You may do it if you wish, but in that case, what the deuce am *I* doing here?"

"He did not mention anything of the sort. We are leaving in a week. That was all settled at the beginning."

"Did he say if the apartment on North Audley is ready?"

"No, he didn't."

"I suggest you ask him."

"You could take the pleasure out of winning a

lottery, Mrs. Irvine," I scolded. "Lord Marndale is just friendly, that's all."

"You don't frighten a filly when you're trying to get the bit in her mouth. Victoria is the burden he means to saddle you with, my girl. Mark my words. There is no point stretching your neck like an angry gander."

"You are mixing your metaphors, Mrs. Irvine. Am I a filly or a gander?"

"A goose!"

Sunday morning we went to church; Sunday afternoon it rained. The gentlemen worked in Marndale's office for a few hours and afterward read the newspapers. I caught up on my correspondence, and we all retired early. In a surly mood I determined to speak to Marndale about the apartment on North Audley Street before he left the next morning. I waylaid him as he was sorting papers in his office in preparation of leaving.

"Did you find time to get around to your apartment house?" I asked.

He looked so blank that I knew it had never entered his head. "I was too busy, but I'll attend to it tomorrow," he said. After a pause he continued, "You are not in a great rush to leave us, I hope? Since you and Vickie are getting on so well . . ."

"I believe we agreed on the duration of my visit. I would like to leave in a week."

He gave a frowning pause. "In a week I'll have some time to spend at Wycherly myself," he said. "I had hoped—"

The breath caught in my lungs. He wanted me to stay till he could be here full-time! The charm of London faded like mist in sunlight as I envisaged the days with Marndale here entertaining Victoria and myself. Then I remembered Mrs. Irvine's warning.

"No, no. I want to get to London before the Season is over," I said brusquely. But I added in a friendlier, jocose manner, "I was happy to give you a hand, but there are limits to my patience, Marndale."

"Of course. I'll get busy and find someone to replace you. Now that is a contradiction in terms," he added, with another of those devastatingly intimate smiles. "One cannot replace the irreplaceable."

Lord Anselm chose that inopportune moment to come blundering in. "Did you get the alterations to the bill—oh, Miss Robsjohn. I was looking for you to say good-bye. Au revoir, rather. I look forward to seeing you in London soon. You forgot to give me your direction."

His hair never looked frizzier or his chin longer. I wished him at Jericho. "Marndale can give you the direction," I replied.

Marndale cast a questioning look on me. He was either thinking I had lied about my former familiarity with Anselm or that I had been encouraging him wantonly. He would think I could love a man like Anselm. He must abhor either my veracity or my taste in gentlemen.

Lady Victoria and Mrs. Irvine came to the door to make their farewells, and the gentlemen left with no further private conversation. Marndale's leave-taking was more than civil but less, somehow, than I had anticipated. I did have the satisfaction, however, of telling Mrs. Irvine that I had spoken to Marndale about leaving and that he knew our plans.

Chapter Nine

On Monday Victoria and I discussed with the Hubbards the preparations for our overnight hiking expedition. I personally viewed this as more of an ordeal than anything else, but it had taken hold of Victoria's imagination, and she considered it a necessary step on her climb to self-dependence. There was no sorrow in my heart when the next day dawned too dark to begin the enterprise. Rain looked imminent, but till it came we spent the morning rehearsing our outdoor skills: building a fire in the stable yard, packing our gear, and so on.

The sky cleared by midafternoon, but I managed to convince her an early-morning start was of the essence, and she was easily diverted to continue her driving lessons instead. The next morning it was pouring rain, and even though the sky cleared shortly after lunch the bush would obviously be too wet to make the outing anything but a misery. When we returned from our driving lesson that day some neighbors had called and were being entertained by Mrs. Irvine in the saloon.

Mr. and Mrs. Everett were friendly, provincial people, whose main interest was political. They wished to discover how Marndale was progressing with some appointment he was trying to procure for their son. We told them he would be home on the weekend, and we would ask him to notify them. Mrs. Everett was curious to learn who Mrs. Irvine and I were and what we were doing at Wycherly, but she expressed her curiosity so genteelly and discreetly that it was possible to misunderstand her and get away with the vague words "friends" and "little visit."

Wednesday, which dawned fair, was the one day Victoria did not want to go on our expedition. "I had thought we would be back from it by Wednesday," she said. "I promised Mrs. Munson I would call with a basket. I have had Cook prepare a basket of food, and I have packed a parcel of baby blankets and things from the attic for the twins. I cannot let her down. A lady's word is her bond, is it not, Jennie?"

"Yes, indeed," I assured her. I was relieved at the reprieve and proud of my charge, too. This was scarcely the same hoyden who had stowed away in my carriage a week before.

When we returned from the Munsons' at noon on that same day, Marndale was there. He had got home earlier than expected and was to stay for the remainder of the week. His first words were to his daughter, but above her head his eyes sought me out with unhidden eagerness. His greeting to me a moment later was flatteringly effusive.

When I quote the words, "Nice to see you again, Jennie. I must say, the country certainly agrees with you," they sound ordinary enough. But their delivery was flattering. A man's eyes do not dart so intensely over a lady's face and linger so long on hers if the words are mere civilities.

There was no mention of Anselm but much talk of Marndale hurrying up his business as he was eager to finish it and be free to spend a little time at home.

"If you have come to visit me, Papa, you have chosen your time badly," his daugher told him. "Jennie and I will be leaving on our outdoor expedition tomorrow morning."

"I made sure you would be back by now."

"No, the weather prevented our going. We leave tomorrow."

Marndale looked a question at me. "Must you?" he asked quietly. Again the words give no notion of the mood. His look spoke volumes of disappointment.

"Is there some special reason you would like us to remain, Papa?" Victoria asked. "If it is important, naturally I shall put off the expedition, but you know Jennie is leaving next week, and I could not undertake it without her."

Marndale was much too clever to reveal any expression of slyness, but I had the sense that his "reason" was an excuse, conceived on the spur of the moment. "As a matter of fact, I do need you, Victoria. I have some important guests coming this weekend. Some members of Parliament and even a few ministers. As my hostess you will be in charge of making them comfortable. I quite depend on you."

"On *me!*" she exclaimed. It would be hard to say whether she was more astonished or pleased.

"You are old enough to take on the duties of my hostess now. It will be excellent practice for when we go up to London next spring."

"Will I sit at the foot of the table and be able to stay up late?" The very nature of her concerns showed she was too young for the job. On the other hand, she was not *much* too young, and the country was a good place for her to begin learning her duties.

"Certainly," he replied.

"Oh, Jennie, this is all your doing! Only a month ago Papa called me a silly goose. You were right as usual. You said if I wished to be treated like an adult, I must act like one, and already Papa is treating me like a grownup. Thank you, Papa." She ran to him and threw her arms around him in a display of childish eagerness. Over her head Marndale gave me a sheepish look.

"Then we may consider the expedition off?" he asked her.

"Postponed till I have performed my duties as hostess." She turned to me. "Could you not stay just one or two days longer, Jennie, and we could have the expedition on Monday, after Papa's guests leave?"

Marndale looked to hear my answer. "Good students should be rewarded for learning their lessons so well, don't you think, Jennie?" he asked.

"If the weather is good on Monday, I shall stay for our outing, but I cannot linger here forever."

We all three talked a little longer. When Victoria dashed off to begin being an adult by telling the housekeeper of her new glory, I had a private word with Marndale.

"Mrs. Irvine will not like my prolonging the visit," I said. "She is eager to be getting on to London. Is the apartment ready?"

"I stopped around the last thing before leaving London. The painters were giving it a final lick and polish. It is practically ready to move into."

"Did you manage to find someone to stay with Victoria?"

"I twisted my cousin Alberta's arm. She has tentatively agreed to come to Wycherly till I can find a suitable companion. It is deuced hard to find the

85

proper sort of lady. Alberta is really much too old, and the half dozen who answered my advertisement were either too young or too sly or too underbred. A man is particular in his requirements for a lady to help him raise his daughter."

"Yes, it must be someone he could trust completely regarding not only character but also social graces. Would it not be better for you to take Victoria to London with you, where you could keep a sharper eye on her and her companion?"

Marndale's head jerked up in surprise at my suggestion. He rubbed his jaw thoughtfully, frowning. He was interested, but something in the idea displeased him. "Do you think it would do?" he asked doubtfully. "It is the question of propriety that bothers me."

"Where is the impropriety in hiring a companion for your daughter? Why should it be more improper in London than here?"

"What would Mrs. Irvine do? Return to Bath?"

The question seemed totally irrelevant. His meaning did not sink in for sixty seconds. "Mrs. Irvine? Good God, Marndale, you cannot think I meant for you to hire *me*!"

It is seldom that one sees the curious sight of a gentleman blushing. Marndale spluttered and blustered a moment, but there was no hope of concealing his error. "As you and Vickie are getting on so famously, I thought ... Actually it would be an excellent idea. You want to go to London, and I want an unexceptionable companion for my daughter." His eyes glowed with approval of the companion he had in mind. "You see now my concern for propriety. With Mrs. Irvine here there is nothing amiss in your visit, but for a gentleman to go hiring a companion for his daughter plus a companion for his daughter's companion—well, it would be bound to raise speculation."

"I should think so. And in any case, I thought you understood that I do not propose to continue in anyone's employment now that I am financially independent."

"You have heard the old saw: Hope springs eternal ... About your friend—Miss Hopkins, is it?" he said, but I think he just wanted to quit the embarrassment of his error. "You mentioned a colleague of yours who might be suitable."

"Yes, Miss Hopkins, but she is no older than myself. Surely you have any number of young female servants. Would it be improper to hire another as companion to Victoria?"

"A companion is in a different category—not a servant, exactly. She is a gentlewoman. More care is required for her reputation."

"Do you not have a housekeeper in London who might play propriety?"

"Yes, but you intimated Miss Hopkins might be too soft to handle Victoria."

"Victoria has improved. And if you were to be on hand on a regular basis, that would be a further incentive for her to behave. Really I think giving her more duties would do the trick. Will you write to Miss Hopkins?"

"Perhaps. I'll think about it a little more. Now I must wash up for luncheon."

At the noon meal Victoria assumed her place at the foot of the table, at the other end of the board from her father. She made a hostessy business of welcoming Mrs. Irvine and myself to the table and inquiring for our comfort. It was really quite amusing to watch her play off her airs and graces.

Immediately luncheon was over Marndale went into his office and remained there till dinnertime. Victoria took her new duties so seriously that she seldom left the housekeeper's skirt tails. She made an occasional foray into her father's study to discover how many guests she might expect and how long they would stay and so on. About the only contribution I made to all her plans was to suggest she keep notes, which she did.

I sat with her in the late afternoon to learn who was coming. It was a short but impressive roster of guests, mostly political gentlemen and their wives.

"How shall I entertain the ladies while the gentlemen work, Jennie?" she asked. "They will be older ladies, you know, so I cannot do anything too strenuous, like riding."

"You could drive them into Chillingfold. Ladies usually like to see the shops and the village."

This meager suggestion was noted down for the first day. "And after that?" she asked.

"They can stroll through the flower gardens and perhaps tour the house." She made two headings, one for fair weather, one for foul.

"I think that takes care of it. They will arrive late Thursday. Whichever day is fine I will take them into Chillingfold, and the other day they can tour the house. Saturday evening Papa is inviting in neighbors for a larger dinner party and some dancing. I must write the invitations and arrange for the musicians. Now, which bedchambers shall I put everyone in? I'll go upstairs and check the rooms."

I tagged along with her for this job. She had her list in hand, jotting down jobs to be done. Make sure the rooms are turned out, fresh linen, flowers in the rooms, and so on. I noticed she had given the Chinese Room, formerly inhabited by Mrs. Irvine and myself, to a Lady Pogue.

"Is there not a Lord Pogue?" I asked her.

"She's a widow. Her husband's name was Sir John Pogue," she answered rather stiffly.

"Not a favorite of yours, I see?"

"No, a favorite of Papa's," she said curtly.

Her sniffy answer alerted me to suspicion. "How old a lady is she?" I asked nonchalantly. "My thinking is that if she is elderly and infirm, she might not want to come to the village with us. You ought to make some other arrangement for her. Perhaps Mrs. Irvine might help to entertain her."

"She is about your age. Thirty or so."

"I am not that old!"

"Oh, well perhaps she is not either. She is Papa's new flirt. Aunt Alice told me she has seen them together in London, but I did not think he would invite her here at this time. It is supposed to be a working visit."

A ball of anger burned inside me. I had no right or reason in the world to be angry, but I was. This was proof positive that Marndale's only interest in me was to provide his daughter a companion. If he was occasionally a little gallant, it was only to divert me and make me think I should be happy in his household. As this was the case he should not have looked so disappointed when Victoria told him our plan to leave on our wilderness expedition.

"She is very well to grass," Victoria mentioned.

"Is she pretty?"

Victoria clamped her lips tight then opened them a fraction to say, "People seem to find her so."

She would have claimed the lady to be an antidote if it were at all possible. I concluded that Lady Pogue was an Incomparable. And a wealthy one to boot. What chance had I against such stiff competition? None, and the only way to save my face was to pretend to like the situation.

"You should be happy, Victoria. Your father has no son, no one to inherit his estate and fortune. He will certainly want to remarry. You should try to get along with his—his friend. She might end up being your stepmother."

"That is exactly what I am afraid of. I shouldn't

mind his remarrying if he married someone *nice*. She is horrid, Jennie."

"What is it you dislike in her?" I was reduced to quizzing a child and felt guilty about it but not guilty enough to desist.

"Everything. She is selfish and a flirt, and ... She makes me feel stupid and young and awkward. A real lady would not do that. *You* never did, even when I was acting stupidly. You always tried to help me, but she only wants to go off with Papa and leave me alone. I wager she would not last one night in the wilderness. She can scarcely be away from her coiffeur and her dresser for an hour."

Elegance was added to the rich beauty's growing list of attractions. That Marndale had invited her, an unattached lady, to a working visit indicated a serious attachment. And that he persisted in the affair in the teeth of his daughter's opposition was as good as a statement of intention to marry the lady. I must pull back a little in my attitude to Marndale, or I would have Mrs. Irvine saying, "I told you so." About the only good news I heard was that Lord Anselm was also to be of the party. He might provide me an escort for the dancing party.

When I went abovestairs to prepare for dinner, I mentioned offhandedly to Mrs. Irvine that a Lady Pogue, flirt of Marndale's, would be of the weekend party.

"Then we might as well leave immediately. I know why you have been hanging on, Jennie. I told you it was no use."

"Nonsense; we will meet all sorts of eminent people, meet them under Marndale's roof, to lend us a note of ton. That cannot do us any harm when we get up to London."

"Lord Eldon and old Bathurst will do us a world of good!" she said in her ironic vein. "An invitation to sit in the visitors' gallery at the House and hear them spout hot air is the best to be hoped for. It is the vain hope of attaching Marndale that makes you cling on like a burr. You're trying to saddle a dead horse, my girl. Lady Pogue is a famous beauty. Her fame spread as far as Bath during her brief fling with Lord Byron."

That made me sit up and take notice. "I doubt he would marry a lady with that sort of reputation!"

"I doubt he will give *you* the time of day when she is around. Did you ask him about the apartment?"

"Yes. It is ready. We shall leave Tuesday afternoon."

"Why not Monday morning?" she demanded, ready for battle.

"Because I have promised Victoria I would give her that cursed wilderness outing. I regret I ever mentioned it."

"So I must sit and twiddle my thumbs for two extra days. I shall be lonely as a rooster at setting time."

"I am sorry, Mrs. Irvine. I truly am."

"Ah, well, at least I shall suffer in luxury."

"You were right all along. I was aiming too high to think to attach Marndale. Lord Anselm is coming to the party, however."

"That ugly creature."

"He can't help the way he looks."

"No, but he could stay home in the dark."

As she was in a cynical mood, I went to my room to prepare for dinner. I took no pains at all with my toilette and regretted it. Lord Anselm was so eager to see me again that he came posting down to Wycherly a day early. He was in the salon with Lord Marndale when Mrs. Irvine and I entered. He leapt to his feet and came pouncing forward.

"Miss Robsjohn! By Jove, it was worth the long

drive to see you again. I was afraid Marndale would cut me out if I gave him a day's head start."

Marndale's lips quirked at this absurdity. His eyes met mine in a brief glance, but he said nothing, nor did I.

A bow was not enough greeting for Anselm. He had to kiss my hand! It gave me a very close look at this poor frizzed hair, and when he raised my hand, his jutting chin brushed it. It would be very difficult to dredge up any strong emotion for Lord Anselm, but at least I felt gratitude for his attention. I could not but notice, however, that Marndale was trying to suppress a grin, Mrs. Irvine a snort, and Lady Victoria a look of pity.

Anselm took up a seat beside me and reverted to his favorite subject: the seminary. "I have had a letter from Mary. She will be leaving school this month, you know. I daresay many of the girls will depart now that you are gone."

"I shouldn't think so. Lady Mary was set to leave in any case. She is seventeen now, I think?"

"Yes, quite the young lady, but not old enough to make her debut. I shall keep her at home for another year to ripen her."

"And how was London?" I asked, to cut short his seminary prattle.

That made up our conversation till dinner was announced.

Chapter Ten

The gentlemen spent the evening and next morning in the study, and I helped Lady Victoria arrange for the arrival of the guests. I was happy to learn the routine, in case I should one day be mistress of a grand house. Great care was taken for the comfort of not only the guests but for that of their servants and cattle as well. The housekeeper outlined the preparations, and Victoria made a list in her book for another visit. With such a redoubtable house-keeper as Mrs. Eadie, Victoria's job was redundant, but it was a useful lesson for her and me.

Lord Eldon, who was usually nursing a headache from an excess of wine, liked dry toast and strong tea before he came down in the morning. "Strong enough for a mouse to walk across it," was the way Mrs. Eadie described the brew. "And Lord Bathurst takes his shave at night. Isn't that odd? His valet won't touch meat, queer lad." She soon tired of Victoria's questions and sent her off to the stable to conspire with the head groom regarding the quantity of hay and oats required.

At three-thirty there was nothing more to do, so we went to our rooms to prepare a fresh toilette for the guests' arrival. With a thought of Mrs. Pogue, my labors were intensive. I fiddled with my hair till I had made a complete mess of it. Mrs. Irvine came to the rescue with a pair of tortoiseshell combs to lift it back from my face. They disappeared against my Titian hair, so I substituted the new length of blue ribbon and ended up looking like a matron trying to masquerade as a schoolgirl.

Mrs. Irvine invented a new compliment for my efforts. "An old hen dressed as a chicken," she said, shaking her head. She more usually calls such efforts mutton dressed as lamb. I removed the offending ribbon.

The day was chilly, but I had had a new sprigged muslin made up in Bath and wore it with a wrap to keep my arms from turning to gooseflesh. Not five minutes after I went below the carriages began to arrive. First came the Eldons, then the Bathursts. Such notables as the Lord Chancellor and the Minister of State should have been enough to put me in awe, but I confess I paid them little heed. It was Lady Pogue, who had nothing to recommend her but a pretty face and a fortune—and a competition for Lord Marndale—who intrigued me. In my eagerness to see her I stationed myself with a view of the window, quite apart from the eminent guests. Lord Anselm came and sat on one side of me, Mrs. Irvine on the other.

E'er long, the lady drove up in a princess's carriage straight out of a fairy tale. It was a dainty blue chaise, heavily trimmed in gilt, driven by four snow white horses. A footman in gold livery held the door for her. Before she alit she handed him an umbrella to prevent the onslaught of Sol for the one-minute walk to the house. I could see at a glance her figure was enviable. She was small, what the gentlemen call a

Pocket Venus, perfect in every dimension. She wore a blue suit and a simple travelling bonnet. Her dainty toes twittered along light as birds.

"By Jove!" Anselm said, smiling fatuously. I was beginning to suspect his admiration of me was no compliment. He was the sort of man who crops out into admiration for all women who are not downright ugly. But of course this one was something special.

Lady Pogue removed her bonnet before being shown in. She needed no introduction to the company. The gentlemen rose and welcomed her while their ladies exchanged grim-lipped nods. I could only stare in dismay at her hair. It was similar to my own in color and cut but brighter, curlier, and more stylish. Her complexion, too, was pale like mine. Her dark eyes and flashing smile added a certain piquance to the whole that was totally lacking in me. I felt like a tarnished silver pitcher, and she a newly polished version of me.

Marndale rushed forward to welcome her with Anselm tagging at his heels like a puppy. "Rita, delighted you could come," I heard Marndale murmur. He held her hand for longer than was necessary. After she had greeted the other guests, Marndale brought her to meet Mrs. Irvine and me.

She offered her hand like a gentleman, a trick I had thought I invented. "Charmed, ladies. Charles has told me so much about you, Miss Robsjohn." I had heard Anselm call Marndale Charles, but I was displeased that she, too, used the familiarity.

"You have the advantage of me, Lady Pogue. I knew you were coming but nothing else about you."

A flash shot out from her dark eyes, but her lips declared it was only amusement. "I am surprised Charles even remembered my name," she said, tossing a flirtatious smile at him.

"By Jove, he is not likely to forget that!" Anselm declared.

This dubious compliment was rewarded with another smile. Anselm latched onto her arm on the spot and drew her toward the sofa. She took my place, but I drew up a chair and sat bobbin. I meant to stick to her like a barnacle and figure out how I could make myself look more like her. I had heard a rumor that rinsing the hair in lemon juice brought out the highlights. I would steal a lemon from the conservatory the first chance that offered.

Some light refreshments were served to welcome the travellers.

"Have you heard anything from Lord Byron lately, Lady Pogue?" Mrs. Irvine asked over her teacup. "I recall there was some talk in Bath last year."

"He has gone to Italy, I believe. We do not correspond," she said icily. Then turning her shoulder on Mrs. Irvine, she spoke to me. "And how is dear little Vickie coming along, Miss Robsjohn? I hear you are a positive wizard with the child."

"We rub along tolerably well."

She looked across the room, where Victoria sat conversing dutifully with the other ladies of the party. "She has needed a firm hand such as you supply. Dick says you ruled that seminary at Bath with an iron fist."

Anselm—Dick—colored up and laughed inanely. His long chin wobbled like a turkey's wattle. "A regular Turk, eh Miss Robsjohn? But very popular with the young ladies."

"And gentlemen, I should think?" Lady Pogue added archly.

"We only taught young ladies," I told her.

"A lady has a life beyond the school room, n'est-ce pas?"

I didn't know whether to be flattered or offended at her manner. It seemed friendly enough but rather insinuating.

"Not this lady," Mrs. Irvine announced. "You

96

would think the sun rose and set on that seminary. Until she had the luck to inherit a small fortune, of course. Then it was a different story."

"I attended the assemblies at the Pump Room," I reminded her.

Lady Pogue gave me a commiserating smile. "The one time I attended the Bath Assembly I was forcibly reminded of a wake. Surely there were better connections to be made. All those young ladies—some of them must have had widowed papas or eligibles brothers, like Dick." She smiled fondly on Anselm. His chin wobbled in appreciation.

Lord Eldon called to Anselm from across the room, and he excused himself. Marndale came to replace him on the sofa. "You neglected to tell me Miss Robsjohn is a beauty, Charles," Lady Pogue scolded, with a playful smile in my direction.

"You wrong me, madam. Surely I mentioned she was quite in your own style."

We two ladies exchanged a calculating stare. Neither of us expressed pleasure at the utterance. "Comparisons are always odious, never more so than when you compare the charms of ladies—especially in their presence," Lady Pogue said, slapping his wrist in a familiar way. "Miss Robsjohn will not continue tending Vickie if you treat her so shabbily."

"Lord Marndale knows I shall be leaving early next week," I said firmly.

Lady Pogue looked guilty. "Now what have I done!" she exclaimed.

"This is not your doing, Lady Pogue," I assured her. "My arrangements were made some time ago."

"And I have been attempting ever since to dissuade her," Marndale joked.

He soon joined the gentlemen, and Lady Pogue turned an inquisitive stare on me. "What is your hurry in leaving, Miss Robsjohn? A gentleman's home makes a formidable base for a lady in your position."

97

I could almost feel my eyes spark in anger. "I beg your pardon!" *My position*, as though I were a light-skirt or a thief!

"Now you must not take a pet, my dear, but a pretty lady with some fortune who wishes to enter society but is not being formally presented must keep her wits about her. You might marry up or down or sideways. Wycherly—or some similar estate—would serve you better than a set of hired rooms in London. Here you will meet only gentlemen of the first stare."

"Jennie has ten thousand. We figured a baronet, tops," Mrs. Irvine announced. My eyes thinned and my nostrils dilated at her outspoken ways.

The lady laughed lightly. "You aim too low, ma'am. I was not presented, and I had only five thousand, but I nabbed a baronet. With the increase in my fortune since Sir John's death, I mean to win a title." Her clever eyes darted across the room, where the four lords had their heads together, too interested in politics to stop talking about it even in company. It was impossible to tell which gentleman she looked at, but Eldon and Bathurst were both married already. Between Anselm and Marndale there was no question which she meant.

"I am not sure I care to marry at all," I said.

Lady Pogue gave a pained frown. "A single lady is severely restricted in society, Miss Robsjohn. If she is pretty, as we are, all the old cats fear she is after their husbands. It doesn't take them long to cook up a scandal and bar her from the best parties. My husband has been dead eighteen months. I mean to marry before the year is out, though I do not relish taking on a young debutante along with a husband. It puts one in the class of older ladies, being a chaperone. Of course, I must be a little sly about my plans." Again she examined the group of gentlemen. I had never seen such a determined expression on anyone's face. From that moment I considered Marndale as well as shackled. Obviously she referred to Lady Victoria as the debutante.

Our conversation was different from what I had expected—more interesting and entirely frank. She was a solicitor's daughter from Surrey. She had married an older gentleman who wanted a son, which she had failed to supply. She had no children. Before half an hour was up, Lady Pogue knew all about me, too, except my age. That I managed to keep quiet, and she was equally reticent regarding how long she had graced the earth.

Our talk was all of eligible partis and where they might be met in London and how to get invitations to the best gatherings. She lauded my having "got an apartment out of Charles," as she phrased it. "You will meet all his pensioners there. Don't think they won't have the ton calling on them! I am always more than polite to noble old relics. I met Charles through his great aunt Sophronia, whom I used to take out for drives when Sir John was alive. He knew her late husband and used to call on her occasionally. Charitable works are a good ploy, too. I shall get you on to the committee for the state orphans in London. Lady Castlereagh is a member. She might even get you a ticket to Almack's if you butter her up. And if that fails you will be prominent at their annual ball at least."

She was a gold mine of information, and I hung on her every word, as keen as Plato's students at the feet of their mentor. I quite forgot that I was in the same room as the Lord Chancellor and the Minister of State. Much good they would do me; but here was a lady who could set me on the path to a first-rate marriage.

"Do you drive?" Lady Pogue inquired during our conversation.

"Certainly."

"Then you must set up a dashing rig. My friend, Lady Lade, will help you there. And you must make a visit to a French modiste," she added, flickering a glance at my gown.

"But I only have ten thousand pounds."

"Spend it. There is no better investment you could make than to look well and mix with the right people."

"But if I spend all my money and *don't* nab a parti . . ."

She shrugged her shoulders insouciantly. "You will. Perhaps even a title." Her eyes glided across the room again. I beheld the monumental chin and frizzed pate of Anselm.

I was taking lessons from the wrong tutor. Lady Pogue, I realized, would marry a sheep or a goat so long as he could advance her social career. That she had shackled herself, while still young, to an elderly gentleman was proof of it. I was made of different stuff. Some of her advice was useful, but I must pick and choose what parts of it to follow.

A little later she mentioned Lady Lade again. "Is that Lettie Lade, the famous whip?" I asked, remembering Victoria's opinion of the lady.

"Yes, we are bosom beaux."

It was Marndale who had warned his daughter that Lettie Lade was bad ton. He would never marry her bosom beau. I began to suspect that the relationship with Lady Pogue was not an honorable one.

At six we went upstairs to make our toilettes. "You'd best wear the bronze gown," was Mrs. Irvine's way of telling me she was bowled over by my competition.

"I cannot. I'll need it for the larger dinner party and dance Saturday evening. What did you think of Lady Pogue?"

"Monstrously pretty, but she's not the lady that

100

would pop into your mind when you met a spring chicken."

"True, but one wouldn't look long at a peacock without thinking of her. She's about thirty, wouldn't you say?"

"Not a day under."

"She is not at all what I thought."

"I thought she'd be more discreet. I hardly knew what to say when she blurted out for the world to hear that she is chasing after a husband as fast as her legs will carry her. Meanwhile, I shouldn't be surprised if she amuses herself with affairs." She pierced me with a gimlet glance. I knew she meant Marndale.

"Her frankness was quite disarming," I said vaguely.

"I doubt she'd be so outspoken if she didn't think you were cut from the same bolt as herself. I noticed the political wives kept a distance from her. I don't think it is a connection you should pursue, Jennie."

"She does know the London ropes, though."

"Give her a good quizzing while she's here, then—"

There was a tap at the door, and Lady Victoria stepped in. She was dressed and ready for the evening, and looked lovely in a pale pink Italian silk gown with her hair dressed in a new fashion. We made a fuss over her toilette; then she said, "What did you think of Lady Pogue?"

"We were just discussing her," Mrs. Irvine replied. "Does she come here often, dear?"

"As often as she's invited. This is her third visit, but she always comes with a party. If it weren't for the respectable company, I would think she is only papa's *chère amie*."

"You should not say such things, Victoria," I felt compelled to object.

"I am officially out of the schoolroom, Jennie. I

101

may now say—in front of friends at least—all the things I only used to think."

Mrs. Irvine listened, and as the expert in sexual chicanery, gave her advice. "If he is sleeping with her, you need not fear he will marry her. A hen that gives her eggs away cannot expect a farmer to buy and feed her. There's an easy way to find out." We both looked with interest. "What we did aboard the *Prometheus* was to put something in the suspect's bed—a feather duster or a dustpan or something that looked as if a careless maid had left it behind, for we didn't want her to suspect us. If the lady complained the next day, we knew she had slept in her own bed. If she did not, then we assumed she hadn't."

"But what if Papa goes to *her* room?" Victoria countered.

"We'll put one in his bed, too. The gentleman really ought to go to the lady's chamber for such assignations. It would be improper to ask her to go skulking along a dark corridor where she might be seen. But with such fast hussies as Lady Pogue, I wouldn't put it a pace past her to be the predator."

In my mind I had an upsetting picture of Marndale creeping down the corridor in stocking feet to slide into Lady Pogue's bed. "That is disgusting! You should not say such things to Victoria, Mrs. Irvine."

"Pooh. She has to learn the ways of the world sometime. And so do you, miss. You were locked up in that school too long. You're turning into a Bath Miss yourself."

"Such tricks as that are fit for a frigate, not a gentleman's home, and certainly not for the ears of his daughter. Shall we go down and see that all is ready for dinner, Victoria?"

Nothing could be told from the seating arrangement, for Bathurst's wife had the seat of honor on Marndale's right hand and Lady Eldon, his left. The rest of us were scattered along the board. At dinner

Anselm sat between Lady Pogue and myself and shared his chin with us both equally. He flirted with the former and discussed Lady Mary and the seminary with me till I told him frankly it was a subject I would prefer to forget.

After dinner Victoria entertained us with a harp recital, poorly executed, and Lady Pogue played the pianoforte while Anselm accompanied her in a very creditable tenor. Lord Eldon confided to me during an intermission that he had an earache. I thought he referred to the music and was surprised at his poor manners, but it turned out his ache had occurred during the trip to Wycherly. He was well along in drink. He and his lady retired early. The rest of us, including Victoria, stuck it out till eleven. The Bathursts and Mrs. Irvine were the next to leave.

I made a leisurely exit and before reaching the staircase Marndale caught me up, as I hoped he would. "Your daughter is performing well," I mentioned.

"She should. She has been practicing the harp for six years. I had hoped we might hear you perform, Jennie."

"I meant performing her social duties."

"Oh, yes, she did us proud. Do *you* sing or play?" I noticed he adroitly turned the conversation back to a more personal line.

"I have long forgotten the few tunes I once knew how to play. I didn't teach music at school but the academic subjects and social deportment."

"I hope you haven't forgotten how to dance. I look forward to dancing with you tomorrow evening."

"That is like riding. Once learned, never forgotten." From the corner of my eye I noticed Lady Pogue waiting for a last word with Marndale. Anselm was amusing her with some foolishness that sent her silver laughter tinkling along the hall. "Lady Pogue plays beautifully," I added, and watched to gauge his reaction.

"Yes, she is a talented lady," he replied. He turned and studied her a moment with a smile of admiration curving his lips.

"I believe she is waiting for a word with you, Marndale. I must not monopolize you."

"Monopolize me?" he asked, staring. "You've hardly said a word to me since I returned!" His tone was not far from sulking.

"What is there to say? It is a very nice party."

"You seemed to find plenty to say to Anselm during dinner."

"Yes, and if I have to say once more that I do not miss the seminary in the least, I shall crown him. One would think I was born and bred at Mrs. Grambly's seminary."

A smile parted his thin lips. "Ah, is that the nature of your conversations? In that case I need not resent it. Lady Pogue rather thought it was something else that interested him."

I bit back the words that Lady Pogue had a one-track mind and said, "If you are so vulgar as to discuss me behind my back, Marndale, you ought to least be civil enough not to carry tales."

"A lady doesn't usually resent hearing that she has caught a gentleman's interest."

We both glanced toward Anselm as we spoke. He intercepted our looks and came forward with Lady Pogue. The lady placed her marmoreal hand on Marndale's arm and began climbing the stairs while lavishing praise on the delightful visit. I heard him tell her that was largely her doing, as she had played so divinely. Piano lessons were added to my list of things to do in London. It branded me as unfinished, not to be able to perform in public.

"A grand party, by Jove," Anselm said. "A change from the seminary, I warrant." I glared. "Now I have displeased you by talking about the school again, Miss Robsjohn. All the same, you must see the advantages to being companion to one lady in her home as compared with herding a whole class of chattering girls."

"I am quite aware of the advantages."

"Yes, indeed. A young lady of Victoria's age is more a friend than a student. The house and stables are completely at your disposal."

"Did Marndale ask you to bend my ear on this score, Lord Anselm?"

"No, truly!" he objected at once, but there was guilt in his pink cheeks.

"You waste your breath. I do not plan to become a permanent guest at Wycherly or anyplace else where there is a young charge awaiting my attention. I have retired from teaching."

"Still, you must miss the girls at the seminary."

We reached the upper landing, where Marndale and Lady Pogue stood a moment, chatting. Marndale overheard my companion's last speech and turned a laughing eye on me as he made his final bow. "If he is as tenacious at his work as he is on this subject, he must be a first-rate assistant," I said in a low breath.

"Why else do you think he is here? His persistence is greatly appreciated at Whitehall. Moreso than at Wycherly, I think, to judge by the scowl you bestowed on him. Good night, Jennie. Sleep well."

I nodded to the others and left, curiously lighthearted. Marndale was not entirely pleased with my conquest of Anselm, and that being the case, I could not be entirely displeased with it.

Chapter Eleven

Friday morning the gentlemen resumed their endless work, and Victoria took the ladies to the village, as the day was fine. She and Mrs. Irvine escorted Ladies Eldon and Bathurst to see the church and a few examples of municipal architecture. Lady Pogue had no interest in anything that did not wear trousers or add to her personal embellishment. I accompanied her. We poked around the drapery shop but nothing was purchased till we entered the milliner's. There she found a soul mate in the French milliner. For half an hour they chattered about ribbons and feathers and flowers till I was bored to flinders. Lady Pogue tried on every bonnet in the shop and finally bought a navy blue glazed poke bonnet with a high crown, which became her famously.

After lunch at Wycherly the gentlemen declared themselves on a holiday and asked us what we would like to do. Mrs. Irvine elected to accompany Lady Eldon and her husband on a tour of the garden. I have mentioned Mrs. Irvine's universal appeal to all the various sorts of humankind. The Eldons were the exception, and I was a little uneasy to think of that mismatched threesome. Lady Bathurst expressed an interest in the library. Lord Bathurst, a glutton for work, had received a red dispatch box from Whitehall and remained behind to answer some letters from Lord Liverpool.

"What do you say you show me how your driving is progressing, Victoria?" Marndale suggested. "You missed your lesson yesterday."

"Very well, Papa," she said. "You will come with us, of course, Jennie," she added, turning her back on Lady Pogue.

"Let us all go!" Lady Pogue exclaimed. "You too, Dick. There is room for all of us in the open carriage."

"It only holds four comfortably," Lady Victoria said at once. "It is not at all a large carriage."

"You go ahead, Rita," Anselm suggested. "I can amuse myself somehow." His eyes, however, moved in my direction in a meaningful way as he spoke.

I feared I would be palmed off with him, but Marndale, seeing my distress, came to my rescue. "This is your opportunity to try out that bay mare you have your eye on, Anselm," he tempted.

"By Jove! I shouldn't mind getting my leg over her. Have you something Rita can ride?"

"Do take my mount. Silver Star is a sweet goer," Lady Victoria smiled demurely.

Lady Pogue appeared interested in this scheme. I already knew from earlier conversation that she was a bruising rider, and apparently horses took precedence even over pursuing Marndale. Of course, she would not take me for serious competition.

I do not think she would have been much amused by our outing, for we had an experience that would not have been to her urban taste. Marndale treated me as an old friend. I wondered that his easy banter wasn't enough to give Victoria a disgust of me. I concluded that either flirting was her father's customary mode with female guests, or he still hoped to con me into becoming Victoria's companion for a whole year. I knew this would please her. All our conversation has not been recorded, but she occasionally let fall wistful hints that she would miss me.

Marndale looked surprised when I took the ribbons for the initial run down the main road. "Victoria has only driven on Willigan's Road thus far," I mentioned.

"Spoken like a native, Jennie," he said. "Already you are familiar with the territory and our peculiar terms for it. Willigan's Road is known on the map as St. George's Road."

"I got the name and the suggestion for using that particular road from Victoria."

Victoria sat beside me on the front bench of the country carriage with Marndale reclining at his ease on the rear seat with a scenic view of our backs. He leaned forward to engage us in conversation, which I found somewhat distracting, although his conversation was mostly with his daughter about minor local doings. A farmer having his barns painted and such things.

When we reached the side road Victoria and I changed places. "Why don't you sit back here with me, Jennie?" Marndale suggested.

"Victoria might need a hand. There is no saying."

"Demmed lonesome back here," he said with a mock sulk.

"Then you must sit up front and judge your daughter's skill.

"No, no! That is not what I was angling for."

I hopped down and bowed him on to the front

perch. "I have always enjoyed solitude, since I had so little of it at the seminary."

"Now that is not a subject I expected you to raise needlessly!" he laughed.

"Good gracious, I am not ashamed of it. It is only that Anselm harps on it so."

"It is certainly not a matter for shame. A lady ought to be proud of looking after herself."

Victoria just smiled at me. "Soon I shall be as independent as Jennie, Papa." She listed her various charity works and her plans for the future.

"If you would give us another month, Jennie, I'd have to buy her a halo," he smiled, but it was obvious he was delighted with the change.

"A halo is like a reputation, sir," I replied lightly. "It must be earned."

Victoria gave the team their head, and all her conversation was suspended while she concentrated on her driving. Marndale watched her for a mile, complimented her a few times, then turned his body at an uncomfortable angle to face me. "Do you ride, Jennie?" he asked.

"I used to. I haven't for a long time." No number of years was given, nor asked for.

"We must work in a ride this weekend."

"I thought, as Victoria lent her mount to Lady Pogue, that you had no ladies' mounts in your stable."

"I'm sure Vickie would be happy to lend you hers. I really ought to get a lady's mount."

I had assumed he meant we three ought to ride and was surprised. "Do, by all means, use Silver Star, Jennie," Victoria said at once. "You may be sure I shouldn't mind *your* using her, when I lent her to Lady Pogue."

Marndale quirked his mobile brows in a meaningful way. It said he realized the lady was no favorite with his daughter. "She is a bruising rider.

109

You need not fear for Silver Star's welfare," is all he said before rattling on to some other nonsense.

There was a near accident when a large pig darted into the road not three yards in front of us. "Stop the horses!" Marndale shouted, and reached across to help Victoria, but she already had them under control. The pig—it was a black-and-white boar the size of a baby elephant—gave us an ugly snort, turned, and strutted off straight into the nearest garden, where he proceeded to root up a bed of flowers.

"Old Mrs. Weldon lives alone there, except for her sister. We'd best give them a hand with Jethro," Marndale said, and leapt down from his perch to chase the boar. As the horses began to graze quietly by the roadside, Victoria and I joined him. My help consisted of trying to shoo the fearsome animal away from the flowers. I have no idea what Marndale's plan was. It seemed to consist of chasing the snorting creature about from side to side, destroying every bloom in sight, while shouting at the top of his lungs and raising the beast's temper. He had succeeded in bringing the boar to a state of hysteria.

"Playing tag with him is only making it worse!" I said.

"We need a rope," Victoria exclaimed. Jethro turned at the sound of her voice, gave her a belligerent glare, and lowered his head to attack. She darted behind Marndale's back and let out a scream. Jethro squealed back, two octaves higher.

"You ladies get back in the carriage," Marndale said.

"Where is Mrs. Weldon's vegetable garden?" I asked. As they were totally at sea in this predicament, I saw I would have to lure the animal to its pen by food. "And where is Jethro's pen?"

"Both out behind the cottage," Marndale replied.

110

"Run back to the carriage, Jennie, and take Vickie with you. I'll try to chase him back to his pen."

I ignored his advice and ran around behind the little stucco cottage, but the garden was hardly well enough along to provide temptation. I knocked at the door and a little old lady with white hair answered. "Jethro's got loose in your garden. Can you give me something to lure him back to his pen?"

"That wretch! I'll lure him," she exclaimed, and grabbed up a broom in one hand, a towel in the other. She dashed out, brandishing the broom and flapping the towel in a way to further excite the animal. I peered into the kitchen and saw a pan on the stove. It held raw potatoes and turnips in water, cut up for dinner. I felt sure she would not mind sacrificing dinner to save her garden and took the pan around to the front. Marndale had the boar cornered, and it would be difficult to say which was more frightened. The pig's eyes were narrowed, its massive head down, and inhuman, even unporcine squeals issued from its mouth. Marndale would take one tentative step forward then two back.

"Clear out before it attacks you, Marndale," I exclaimed. I tossed a potato on the ground a few yards away. Marndale backed off, and the boar subsided to frightened whimpers.

"Here Jethro, nice piggie," I said, pointing to the food.

The boar stood undecided a moment, but its appetite finally won out, and it went after the potato. After that it was but a moment till I had led it by judiciously dropped bits of potato and turnip to the pen. The last potato I tossed to the very rear of the pen. Jethro trotted in after it, and Marndale closed the gate and locked it. Jethro gobbled down the food and looked to me hopefully for more.

"I'll have that wretch butchered before the week

is out," Mrs. Weldon exclaimed, and flourished her broom futilely "Let me see what damage he's done."

"You shouldn't have left his gate ajar," Marndale told her.

"No, and my foolish sister shouldn't be eighty years old and senile either, but she is. I've told her not to feed Jethro, but she likes to feel useful. She's as much use as a toothache." She grumbled her way around to the front, and we examined her garden.

"Most of these can be replanted. If you get them in right away, they should survive," I said, hoping to console her.

She examined the ruined greenery with a few flowers and buds trodden into the mud. "To hell with them. I'll plant clover, and let my Jennie keep it mowed." I might have known her cow would be named Jennie! "Well, thank you for your help, Lord Marndale. Lucky you happened along. Not that you were much use. Who is this young lady?" she added, turning a penetrating eye on me. "She is the one who saved my bacon. Heh heh. There is a little pun for you. I've seen this young lady driving with Lady Victoria, have I not?"

Marndale introduced me to her. "You must be a farmer's daughter, though you don't look like one. Your fine city ladies would have no notion how to handle an escaped boar. They're good for nothing but making faces in their mirrors and chasing after the gentlemen. You're looking after little Lady Victoria, are you? Can I give you a cup of tea for your trouble?"

She never bothered waiting for answers but continued a monologue. We declined her offer to tea and returned to the carriage. "She's a crusty old lady," I mentioned.

"Yes," Marndale said with an innocent eye. "She used to be the mistress of the dame school in the village. I'm surprised she needed any help."

"She's over seventy, Papa!" his daughter pointed out. She was unaware of any undercurrents in the conversation, and I was happy to leave her in that unenlightened state.

"Would you like to see Munson's twins?" was Victoria's next suggestion. Marndale's land cut at an angle, running parallel to the road, with some of his tenants accessible by another little side road.

"I have seen them. I called to congratulate Munson the day they were born. A newborn is not a thing of beauty."

"Oh, Papa, they're beautiful now!" she insisted. "You must see them. They're called Peter and Paul, after the apostles. Mrs. Munson let me watch her bathe them. She lets me hold Peter, but Paul likes Jennie better. Do come. I wish I had thought to bring something. With all our privileges, you know, we ought to think of those in need."

"My tenants are not in need!" he objected.

"Now don't get your tail up your back, Papa. I only meant some food while Mrs. Munson is so busy and not feeling any too stout after her lying in."

"I don't have a tail! Where do you pick up these vulgar expressions," he grumbled. To her credit she did not betray Mrs. Irvine, nor did I.

"Let us go and see them," she said. "You know you are only sulking because Jennie caught the boar, making you look no how. I told you she can do anything. I learn something new every time I go out with her. Today I learned how to handle a wild boar. I do wish she would stay longer."

"One does not discuss a person who is present as if she were absent, Victoria," I said in my most schoolmistressy voice to stop her praise. Really I felt quite foolish though not entirely displeased. Marndale was studying me with disconcerting frankness.

"Miss Robsjohn is an example to us all," he said.

113

"But I fear she will be the first to tell us that one does not argue with a lady, and she has taken the decision to go to London."

"Couldn't I go, too, Papa?" she asked. "I could stay with you. You could hire me a companion, and I could go on meeting Jennie at least."

He just stood a moment, thinking. "That is something I have been considering," he said, and we set off for Munson's.

Mrs. Munson was now up and about her business. She welcomed us like old friends, though she still bore a little restraint in front of Marndale. "This is who you have come to see, I fancy," she said, leading us to the cradle in the corner of the kitchen where the twins were lying side by side, as like as eggs on a plate.

"May I hold Peter?" Victoria asked rather shyly.

"He'd take a pet if you didn't. You help yourself to Paul, Miss Robsjohn. Two sons! I wish I had a daughter to give me a hand with the housework, but all I am good for is sons. This makes four." She had two older lads of six and seven who were attending the village school.

Victoria and I each took up our favorite and made those strange gurgling sounds that women make over babies. Marndale said a few words to the fond mother, but his eyes often travelled to the twins. I wondered what was in his mind. How ironic that he should have had a daughter when a son was of great importance to him and Mrs. Munson should provide her husband a steady stream of sons when she wanted a daughter. But there is no arguing with Fate.

Before we left he came forward and peered down at the boys. There was such a look of longing on his face and such tenderness as he studied them. I saw a side of him I had not seen before. "Very handsome," he said over his shoulder to the mother. His voice was strange; not unsteady exactly, but I knew he was deeply moved.

I noticed a gold coin sitting on the table when we left. I doubted very much it had been there when we entered.

"Aren't they beautiful, Papa?" Victoria said. "I wish I could have a baby brother."

"But would you want the stepmother that is an integral part of the arrangement?" he asked, trying to make light of it. Some air of distraction still hung about him, though.

She gave her father a bold look. "I shouldn't mind if you let me have some say in the choosing of her."

"Very well then, you find yourself a stepmama, and I shall tend to the rest of it."

"I daresay Sir John Pogue would have liked a son," the sly girl mentioned ever-so-casually. "Lady Pogue must be unable to have children. She was married for nearly ten years and gave her husband no children at all."

Marndale gave her a knowing look. "Pity, when you are so fond of the lady."

"Oh, I have nothing against her as a friend, Papa. She is very pretty."

We stopped for an ice in the village, and Victoria drove us home without incident. It was her second foray onto the main road, and she acquitted herself well. "This carriage is now officially yours, Vickie," he said, when we reached home.

"Oh, but I wanted a green Tilbury, Papa, with a white team."

"A white team is pretentious. It is looking for attention and admiration—fitter for a lightskirt than a lady. As to the green Tilbury, I have no objection to your painting this rig green, if you wish."

No one mentioned Lady Pogue's white team, but I knew by Victoria's grin as she flicked the whip and led the team to the stable that she remembered

115

it. I think it occurred to Marndale, too, as I noticed a little flush creep up his neck. As we went to the door, he glanced at me and smiled sheepishly. "I forgot," he murmured.

"It is not only liars who require good memories."

"We can't all be perfect. Even you, Jennie, have your flaw." Naturally I looked with interest to hear how I fell short of perfection. "You make your visits much too short," he said. While I stood gazing he took my arm and said, "Shall we have a look at the roses?" We strolled arm-in-arm around to the terraced garden. Mrs. Irvine had left, under what circumstances I trembled to think, but the Eldons were still there.

It was not to the roses that he led me but to a paved court edged in dense yews. I sat on a rock-hard stone bench; Marndale remained standing, smiling down at me in the most delightfully familiar manner. I hardly knew what might come next, but his wish for privacy, and now that smile, made my heart thump and my hopes soar.

"Congratulations," he said, after a long look.

Surely even a marquess did not begin a proposal of marriage in such a self-congratulatory way. "For what?"

"Handling Jethro," he said, and threw his head back in unrestrained laughter. "You were *formidable*, Miss Robsjohn." He gave the adjective the French pronunciation. "Anselm is right, even the beasts of the field obey you."

"Jethro obeyed his appetite for turnips and potatoes. It is all in knowing what motivates the animal."

He held out both hands and drew me up from the bench. "And how would you handle the animal with . . . different appetites?" he asked. The glow in his eyes told me what appetite this human animal was about to indulge.

116

"That would depend entirely on what motivated him, as I said."

"Really, Miss Robsjohn!" he said, and pulled me into his arms. A deep chuckle sounded in my ear, as he placed his face against mine. "Surely you do not suspect me of dishonorable intentions! I saw at the Laughing Jack how you handle that breed."

Never have such pedestrian words sounded so loving. His voice was soft and gentle, and when he raised his head, he was wearing an expression akin to that he wore when he looked at the Munson twins. He might as well have been declaring his undying devotion. Our eyes locked in a long, searching gaze. Then his head lowered, and his arms tightened around me.

At that promising moment the demmed Eldons decided to return. We jumped apart as if we had been plotting treason. "Ah, Marndale," Lord Eldon said, while his lady examined me as if I were a piece of dirty muslin, "time for a glass of something wet, eh? It is hot work, looking at flowers in the sun." Our Lord Chancellor, the human sponge, wanted more wine.

We all entered the house together, and the magic moment passed without coming to fruition.

Chapter Twelve

In my simplicity I thought our visit at Wycherly was going splendidly. I reckoned without the naval widow. What must Mrs. Irvine do but make a cake of herself in front of the whole party. I knew by her dark brow when I went upstairs to change for dinner that something had gone amiss, and with the greatest misapprehension inquired what ailed her.

"I have had a wretched afternoon," she scowled. "And it is all because of the Eldons. I am surprised Marndale is entertaining that lot, for Lord Eldon, besides drinking a good deal too much, is against every sort of reform. His views would have been thought dated in the dark ages. He is against the abolition of slavery, Catholic emancipation, and all *for* throwing unfortunate souls into jail for debt."

"We are not here to discuss politics," I foolishly replied.

Politics was the subject of discussion after dinner, however, and though it was Lord Eldon who was responsible for dredging up the old quarrel, Mrs. Irvine jumped at the chance to have a go at him. The Eldons had recently been home to Newcastle-upon-Tyne and were deriding the condition of the roads. "What we ought to do is empty the jails and debtors' prisons and set those layabouts to earning their keep by working on the roads," he said with a challenging eye to my chaperone.

"First we would have to feed and clothe them properly to give them strength for the job," she said with an angry twitch of her shawl.

"It is not lack of food that has weakened them but lack of character. It is easier to steal than do an honest day's work, but it doesn't put muscles on a man."

"You, being a politician, would know about stealing," she shot back, heedless of the other politicians in the room.

Marndale sat up, his back as stiff as a ramrod, and flashed a warning glance at her. She was not looking at him, and he next stared at me. My ingenuity abandoned me.

He said to Lord Bathurst, "Mrs. Irvine's late husband was in the navy. He was killed at Trafalgar. Did you know Lord Bathurst used to be lord of the admiralty, Mrs. Irvine?"

This awkward attempt at changing the subject failed miserably. "Of course I knew it," she said, still glaring in Eldon's direction.

Lord Eldon also ignored the interruption. "Yes, we're good at stealing—from the rich to give to the poor, like Robin Hood," he said. "I know your views on letting debtors run free, Mrs. Irvine, but not paying one's debts is a form of stealing. If we let them off scot-free, no one would pay his debts."

"If you lock a man up for owing a little money, how is he ever expected to repay it?"

"Paying is the last thing they are interested in. It is the rich who have to support them while they

119

are incarcerated. Don't think we do it for the good of our pocketbooks."

"It's news to me if *I* am rich, but I pay my taxes, to say nothing of the road tolls, along with the tax you put on journals and I don't know what else."

"The needs of the nation must be paid for," he said grandly. "Prisons must be paid for. Wars must be paid for."

"And especially our prince regent's improvidence must be paid for. His debts could have financed the war instead of making us a laughingstock amongst civilized nations with his extravagance, to say nothing of his women."

"A prince cannot be expected to live like a pauper," Eldon announced. "And where do you think your late husband's pension comes from?"

"Obviously not the same rich coffer as your income, sir! My quarterly pittance wouldn't pay your wine bill for a week."

I darted a worried glance at Marndale. To inveigh against political chicanery was one thing. For Mrs. Irvine to sink to personal slander was really going too far. "Speaking of wine, you were going to test the new claret I laid down, Eldon," Marndale said. "It is in my study. Shall we try it?" He rose and helped Eldon from his chair.

Wine, it seemed, was the one thing that could turn Eldon's attention from a fight, and he rose on unsteady legs to go to the study. Lord Bathurst and Anselm went with them, casting unhappy looks at Mrs. Irvine over their shoulders.

Lady Eldon added her cold stares. "I believe I shall go upstairs," she announced.

"Yes, it's been a long day," Lady Bathurst agreed, and together they went from the room.

We four younger ladies were left alone. Lady Pogue gave a shake of her head. "You really ought

120

not to have said that, Mrs. Irvine. Charles was not pleased with that little outburst."

"No more I should, which is not to say I was wrong."

"The Eldons are not leaders of the ton," Lady Pogue continued. "Old Bags came from nowhere and was made a baron for his work in Parliament. The family is not noble by any means. His wife was only a rich banker's daughter, but she is not someone who can be insulted with impunity either. She has the ear of Lady Castlereagh. Almack's, you know . . . Lady Eldon is probably complaining to Lady Bathurst this minute. The Bathursts are unexceptionable. Their ancestors go back to Norman times. Perhaps if you apologized to Lady Eldon . . ."

"You might as well ask a stone to bark," I said. "Mrs. Irvine was right, and therefore she cannot possibly apologize, though that slur on Eldon's drinking was out of place."

"I'm sorry I didn't say more," Mrs. Irvine declared. "I should have suggested he tax wine."

"He likes his bottle," Lady Pogue conceded. "He is considered a man of slow but sound judgment. I'll just go up and see if I can smooth his lady's ruffled feathers," she said graciously, and left. I believe she did not want to be found talking with us heathens when the others returned.

"Don't tell her I'm sorry!" Mrs. Irvine called after her. She soon went abovestairs herself. Victoria and I lingered, but the gentlemen remained away a long time. I did not want it to look obvious that I was hanging on in hopes of a few words with Marndale, so I went up, too.

Between my little argument with Mrs. Irvine when I went upstairs and worries over what Marndale might think, I did not sleep easily. My main concern was that her outburst would lessen his feelings for me. Surely he had been on the very edge of an offer in the garden.

I was not looking forward to breakfast the next morning, but when I went down it was only Marndale who was at the table. I was not so optimistic as to expect a proposal over the toast and jam. He smiled when I appeared, but a first glimpse of his frowning face told me what preyed on his mind, too.

"Good morning, Jennie," he said. "Did you sleep well?"

"I slept badly, and I think you did, too." He had purple smudges below his eyes. "You look a little fagged, Marndale."

"Someone had to drink Eldon under the table so he would forget last night's debacle."

"Much good that will do! His wife will be sure to remind him. She left very shortly after her husband with a pretty sharp look at Mrs. Irvine. But I would hardly call that little contretemps a debacle!"

"True, with Rita's help, utter disaster was avoided. She mentioned last evening that she tried to explain to Lady Eldon, making much of Mrs. Irvine's being a war widow."

"Last evening?" Lady Pogue, it seemed, had no reservations about hanging on forever. She must have returned below after pacifying Lady Eldon. From the looks of Marndale's face, he must have been drinking for hours. How long had Lady Pogue waited for him?

"I had a word with her before I retired," he said. "And I would appreciate it if you would have a word with your chaperone. Put a clamp on that woman's tongue, if you can."

My hackles were already up on Mrs. Irvine's behalf. That casual mention of Rita's help did nothing to smooth them. "I hope Lady Pogue did not apologize! We expressly asked her not to when she so

122

officiously went chasing after Lady Eldon. Mrs. Irvine was right, and I am surprised you are so concerned for the good opinion of a dinosaur like Lord Eldon."

His lips moved unsteadily to repress a smile. "True, he is firmly rooted in the eighteenth century, but he is influential for all that. Bathurst and I have been given the sensitive task of updating his views, primarily softening his resistance to parliamentary reform. That is why the Eldons are here."

"Would it not help if you could keep him sober?"

"We are not miracle workers. Eldon likes his wine, but he is a hard worker."

Mrs. Irvine came down while we were still alone and said to Marndale, "I daresay I set the cat amongst the pigeons last night. Sorry, Marndale, but there was no bearing that old snuff dipper's taunts. He said that about the debtors on purpose to vex me. He knew my views, for we had already whipped that horse in the afternoon."

"Apology accepted, ma'am, but I would appreciate it if you would keep your distance from him if you cannot keep your temper."

"Would you like me to leave?" she asked.

To my astonishment Marndale did not immediately object. He liked the idea of her leaving. Did he think for one minute I would remain behind without her? He intercepted my frozen face and said, "No, no! That was not my meaning. I'll keep him busy. It will only be for another few days."

"Perhaps we ought to go, Mrs. Irvine," I said.

"Victoria would be mighty disappointed to miss her outdoor adventure," my chaperone mentioned. "I was thinking we could take that hike while the guests are here."

"Oh, but Victoria is acting as Marndale's hostess!" I objected at once. Thoughts of the grand dinner and dancing party floated in my head.

"The arrangements have all been made," she said. "If it needs only a lady to sit at the end of the table, any of the others could do it. Lady Pogue or Lady Bathurst." She did not mention Lady Eldon for the job.

I took a peek at Marndale. He showed no emotion at all in Mrs. Irvine's scheme, either for or against. I was prepared to let the matter drop. "Just don't listen to Lord Eldon if he taunts you again," I suggested.

"I'll try, but it is hard to ignore a jackass braying in your ear."

"Jennie will teach you the trick," Marndale said with a teasing smile. "She manages to ignore me. Just try to be patient, ladies. After lunch I will be taking the gentlemen to call on some local worthies. Soon our company will be gone, and I promise you I shall repay you for your forbearance. Ah, here is Victoria!"

She took her place at the table and said, "I am trying to entertain your guests, Papa, but they don't want to do anything. I have suggested all sorts of things. Tours and drives and walks. They just want to sit home and read and talk. Perhaps the ladies are too old—except for Lady Pogue, and she has already arranged to have another ride on Silver Star today. We might as well have our driving lesson, eh Jennie?"

Breakfast was fairly enjoyable, but it was cut short. As soon as the shuffle of feet beyond the door announced the arrival of the Eldons and Bathursts, I got hold of Mrs. Irvine and led her off. Whatever of her food was not still on her plate was in her throat. Curt nods were exchanged as we met the others entering. Lady Pogue was not with them. But then I already knew she had had a late night. We went upstairs to wait for Victoria.

"I believe I'll go for that driving lesson with you,

Jennie, for I don't mean to sit like a jug glaring at Lady Eldon all morning," my companion said.

"That might be best."

In about ten minutes Victoria came tapping at the door. Her pretty little lips were down at the corners. "What a horrid party this is turning out to be," she said. "I'll be glad when they leave. Though to tell the truth, I dislike to see Papa go off to London with Lady Pogue. I tried your little stunt about putting the coal scuttle in her bed last night, Mrs. Irvine, and she didn't say boo about it. She must have slept with Papa."

You may imagine my reaction to this, especially after that episode in the garden. Fortunately fury held my tongue frozen, but Mrs. Irvine answered unconcernedly. "I own I am surprised. I made sure he would go to her room. The hussy is certainly legging it after him very hard."

My heart was banging in my breast. He had sat smiling so warmly at breakfast, promising a reward for our forbearance. If he thought I would forbear this lechery, he had another thing coming. To flaunt his affair, with the dinosaur Eldon in the house, to say nothing of his own daughter and me! Hanging was too good for him. Every instinct urged me to pack up my bags and leave the house on the instant. I would not be able to see the man without scratching his eyes out. Yet how could I explain my sudden decision to Victoria and Mrs. Irvine?

"I'll get my bonnet and pelisse," Victoria said, and rose. She had been saying something to me, but in my state of distraction I hadn't heard a word.

"No!" I exclaimed. She looked over her shoulder, surprised. "We—we have to leave, Victoria," I said, and looked a warning to Mrs. Irvine.

"Oh, no!" Victoria exclaimed, her face clenched in chagrin.

"No, Jennie," Mrs. Irvine said. "You are thinking of Marndale's little warning to me. I thought nothing of it. I did not take offense in the least." She turned to explain to Victoria. "Your papa was not happy with my little outburst last night, but I don't think he wants us to leave."

"No, he doesn't!" she said emphatically. "In fact, he said that after the Eldons and the Bathursts leave, we will all—"

No mention of Lady Pogue leaving! If he thought my chaperone and I were going to provide a respectable window dressing for his affair with Lady Pogue, he was very much mistaken. "We really must be going. Something has come up," I said, and jumped up on the instant to open the clothes press and started grabbing my gowns from their hangers.

"But the wilderness excursion! We haven't had that yet," Victoria said, close to tears. "Where are you going? I don't understand. What has happened to upset you, Jennie?"

"Nothing. It is just past time we were getting on. Marndale is too polite to say so, but he would prefer that we leave."

Mrs. Irvine sat with her tongue between her teeth, looking and thinking. When she spoke her usual common sense was revealed. "If you just want to keep me out of Eldon's way, let us have our excursion now. Victoria has made all the plans for the dinner party and dance."

"I couldn't let Papa down," Victoria said. "This is the first time he has ever asked me to help him."

"It won't be the last," Mrs. Irvine assured her. "And you already have helped him. You have made all the arrangements."

"Victoria is right," I said severely. "This is not the time for the excursion."

"But when will we have it?" Victoria asked, close to tears.

"I don't know, Victoria. Perhaps some time . . ."

I could hardly think, much less speak, for the pictures swirling around in my head. Lady Pogue,
slipping down the hall in her nightdress. Was
Marndale listening for her at the door, waiting to
draw her into his arms?

"Could you wait a little longer if we went on the
excursion today?" Victoria asked.

"Yes. No—I don't know."

"We'll do it today and be back Sunday afternoon.
You can leave for London on Monday. Will that do,
Jennie? It will keep Mrs. Irvine and the Eldons
apart."

I didn't know whether I wanted to go with her or
not. I truly did not want to disappoint Victoria. Perhaps some mean corner of my heart wanted to vex
Marndale, to show him I had more influence over
his daughter than he. I would show him as well
how little I thought of his dancing party. I would
prefer a night in the wilds. Perhaps I even wanted
a last possibility of seeing him again. In any case,
I agreed.

"Be sure you ask your papa first," Mrs. Irvine
reminded Victoria as she ran from the room.

"This is a harebrained notion, our running off as
if we were criminals," she said when we were alone.
"It is none of your concern if Pogue hopped into his
bed last night."

"That is not of the least interest to me one
way or the other. You know why we must leave—
because you cannot hold your tongue in polite company."

"I might in *polite* company. Eldon is another
matter. And that is not the real reason for this mad
dash. I daresay Marndale won't let his daughter
leave at this time."

Victoria was soon back. "Papa thinks it an excellent idea, Jennie."

My sinking heart told me I was disappointed. I

had thought he would forbid it. Had he not said he was looking forward to dancing with me? But perhaps I misunderstood. "He means just a daylong excursion, with us returning for the dance?" I happened to look out the window and saw the sky was threatening rain. "I doubt we could sleep outdoors tonight. The sky is like lead."

"No, Papa mentioned that, but he says the weather is clearing. We have arranged that Lady Pogue will be his hostess for dinner. That is probably what he really wants anyway," she added with a pout. "He says we may stay overnight."

Frost settled over my heart and chilled my reply. "Then you must speak to the Hubbards and prepare yourself for the outing," I said, and began my own preparations as soon as she left.

Mrs. Irvine grouched as she changed into her oldest gown and most comfortable walking shoes. "I little thought when you talked me into going to London that I would end up in the bush like a wild Indian."

"If you hadn't insulted the Lord Chancellor, we would not be going into the bush." That brought her grumblings to a halt.

The Hubbards already had a spotted mare called Belle loaded up with cooking utensils and so on ready in the stable. They were a young, rough couple, but full of good-natured raillery. Hubbard wore a misshapen hat pulled low over his eyes. His wife was a buxom girl with blond curls and lovely blue eyes. By the time the necessary food supplies were assembled we three ladies, dressed in our shabbiest outfits and sturdiest boots and worst bonnets, were eager to be off.

I rather thought Marndale might excuse himself from the meeting for a moment to say good-bye and add some warnings for our safety, but he did not feel it necessary to do so, and we did not leave any message for him either.

Lady Pogue and Lord Anselm came to the stable just as we were leaving. She looked lovely in a scarlet riding habit and black bonnet. I mentioned to Anselm that I was a little surprised at his being allowed to escape work.

"I am only a very small cog in the machine," he explained. "A sort of amanuensis. They will decide what is to be done, and I will write up their report when I return."

I was a little piqued that Lady Pogue was stealing Anselm as well as Marndale. He, at least, I had thought safe from her clutches and a possible entrée into society for me when I reached London. When he asked me to save him a waltz, however, and I told him I would not be home, his genuine regret cheered me.

Chapter Thirteen

As we trudged into the bush I thought much of my future plans. It was impossible now to take an apartment from Marndale. I wouldn't take anything from him, not the lint from his pocket or the steam from his porridge. In fact, the whole idea of London was becoming a bore. If Lady Pogue's and Marndale's behavior was typical of noble carrying-on, I wanted no part of it. I would return to Bath, where my small fortune would go a deal further than it would in London. The saving would allow me to set up a Tilbury or phaeton, and I had developed a strong desire to do so since driving with Victoria. I did not mention these plans to either of my companions, however. Some corner of my heart still wanted to go to London and be tortured by seeing Lady Pogue and Marndale making cakes of themselves.

Deep in thought I lost all track of time, but eventually I began to feel the strain of long walking. As we advanced the meadow turned to brush, the brush to a spinney; then it deepened to a forest. It was quite lovely at first in the shady green light, and to make up for my long silence, I made much of the fresh, piny scent, and the occasional bit of wildlife in the form of birds, rabbits, badgers, and field mice. Some wild flowers spotted growing in a shadowy glen demanded a few lines of Wordsworth.

A violet by a mossy stone
Half hidden from the eye!

"That there's not a violet, miss," Hubbard told me. "A violet's blue or purple. That one's yaller. It's what we call a fairy's slipper."

"I was quoting from a famous poet, Hubbard."

"He can't be much of a poet if he don't know a violet from a fairy's slipper. And besides, it don't rhyme."

"The violet was meant to refer to a country girl growing up away from society and unappreciated. An analogy, you see."

"Like my Meg," he said, casting a calf's eye at his wife.

"Watch who you're calling an alogy, Hubbard!"

"Now who's been writing you poems, Meg?" he joked. He and his wife had a loud laugh at this romantic exchange of pleasantries.

"I'm hungry," Mrs. Irvine announced. "When do we stop to eat?"

"When we have appreciated a little more of the wilderness," I told her.

"This is not what I'd call wilderness. I can still see smoke from Wycherly's chimbleys," Hubbard said. "I go farther than this on my afternoon stroll."

"So this is where you peel off to!" Meg exclaimed.

"Just having a peek to see if you're meeting poets by them mossy stones."

"Oh you!" She gave him a playful swat that sent him reeling.

"They're newlyweds," Victoria explained in an aside.

A loud clap of wings and a swish of leaves in a tree overhead caught our attention. "That there's a partridge!" Hubbard exclaimed. We watched it soar into the air.

"Lovely!" I exclaimed. No quotation came to mind.

"Don't I wish I'd had my gun cocked," Hubbard said with a regretful shake of his head.

"We are not here to slay wildlife but to admire its beauty," I informed him. "If we had fresh snow, I could point out how one tells what animals have passed by their tracks," I mentioned to Victoria. Underfoot the ground was slippery with fallen needles withered to brown, and dead leaves.

"We don't need no snow to tell the air is growing black with midges," Meg Hubbard said, batting them away from her face.

Deep in the forest the air was thick with insects, mostly midges. "Here is how we take care of that," I said. I had taken the precaution of getting some cheese cloth from Wycherly, which we arranged over our bonnets and tied under our chins. This held off the midges but hampered vision. Vision did not hamper Hubbard's lessons, however. He knew the birds by their song.

"The songbirds of summer have arrived," I said. "Listen to that sweet warbler."

"That there's not a warbler, miss. It's a chiff-chaff," he told me.

"I know a willow warbler to see it," I objected. I was the teacher! What did this ignorant servant know?

"Chiff-chaff," he repeated. "Listen now. Two notes, that's what you're hearing. That there's a chirp, not a warble."

"But how cleverly he changes his two notes."

"Aye, the chiff-chaff chirps sweet, but she don't warble."

Hubbard continued to correct my every assertion. Willow-wrens were not wrens but dunnocks. My blackcaps were his garden-warblers. "Do you see a black cap on that bird?" he demanded.

"No, I see a brown cap, for it is the female of the species."

"Don't you see the bits of green and yaller on it? Garden-warbler," he said in a voice that brooked no argument.

"Hubbard is not wearing his veil. That is why he sees more clearly," I mentioned to Victoria, for I did not want her to get the idea I was as ignorant as I felt.

When Hubbard announced, "Sedge-warbler," I was sufficiently cowed that I did not deny it. "A bit of a comic, that fellow. Only hear how he mimics the blackbird. I daresay we're nearer his nest than he likes. He's serenading us so we won't find the wee ones. We'd best step careful." I paid little heed to this and continued forging ahead.

A little further along Mrs. Irvine stumbled into a rabbit hole and wrenched her ankle. "It's this curst cheese cloth that makes everything blurry," she complained. She gamely insisted we carry on, but it was clear that every step pained her. Hubbard removed part of Belle's pack and put it over his own shoulders to allow Mrs. Irvine to ride on the back of the saddle horse. I believe she had an even more miserable morning than the rest of us, but she did not complain except of hunger. "I wish I had finished my breakfast. I am ravenous."

"This must be excellent for the character, for it is so very miserable," Lady Victoria said weakly. Glancing at her, I noticed the child was strained with fatigue, or perhaps it was only the cheese cloth that painted her face white.

133

I was bone weary myself by that time and began looking about for a suitable place to stop. We wanted a fire to make tea, and that required a clearing to prevent setting the forest ablaze.

It was impossible to get much idea of the weather in the forest, with treetops forming a more-or-less impenetrable roof over our heads. I only knew that I was deuced hot, with perspiration beading under my hat and veil and dripping down on my forehead. It was the pattering of drops on the leaves above that alerted us to rain, for no water had gotten through yet.

"This is all we needed," Mrs. Irvine moaned.

Turning to solace her, I did not notice that the ground before me was swampy. I sunk to my ankles in black, muddy water and emitted an unladylike oath.

"I warned you to look sharp for the water," Hubbard crowed. "Your sedge-warbler wouldn't be nesting far from water, though he will move a ways off from it upon occasion."

"I thought your father recommended this route," I said to Victoria.

"He wouldn't know it is so wet. He never comes here himself."

"He has sent us picnicking in a bog."

She gave me a rebuking look. "I expected more fortitude from you, Jennie," she said primly, and began a dainty detour around the boggy bit of ground. I followed, firmly put in my place.

I determined not to let my ill-humor with Marndale ruin this outing, which had so long been looked forward to. "We are all tired. It is time to stop for tea," I announced. "Let us find a clearing."

"A clearing? We'll be soaked alive if we get out from under these branches," Hubbard grinned.

The others heaved a universal sigh of relief that we were to rest at least. Right on top of it came a mighty crack of thunder. Belle reared up on her hind legs, leaving Mrs. Irvine sitting in the water cursing like a Tar while the nag bolted. Pans and pots rattled at Belle's sides as she fled. But the swamp provided soft falling, and I knew Mrs. Irvine was not seriously hurt at least. Recovering the horse was more important.

The wretched animal cantered forward amidst the trees, showing us a bold swish of her tail as she fled with all of us who were still able-bodied in pursuit. She ran till she came to a stream, which she leapt across only to stumble in the bog on the other side. She rolled over on her back, whinnying fiercely. I felt in my bones we had crippled one of Marndale's nags, to put the cap on this wretched day. On top of the rest the bag of food the animal was carrying was soaked. Water streamed from the oilskin bag.

Hubbard and his wife helped the wildly whinnying mare up and out of the mire. Her eyes rolled alarmingly, and her coat was dripping with black water and covered with bits of decaying vegetation. We were all in a similar state by the time Victoria and I went back and pulled Mrs. Irvine from the bog. I never felt so uncomfortable and bad-tempered in my life. Our shoes and stockings were squelching. Sodden skirts and petticoats flapped about our ankles, hampering every step.

"We've run aground now surely," Mrs. Irvine declared.

"We should be so lucky as to have hit dry land! I hope you are carrying the tea, Hubbard," I said through clenched teeth.

He was enjoying my disgrace thoroughly. "Aye, and a morsel of bread. My Meg'll build us a bit of a fire. I'll just shoot us a hare and skin her and we'll eat."

"That grizzly performance will hardly be conducive to eating."

"I thought we was roughing it."

135

"Bread and tea will do if that is all that remains of our food," I said. Another ominous rattle of thunder sounded, but the rain did not penetrate our leafy roof.

"Nay, you call this roughing it?"

Victoria looked at me askance. "I thought we were to live at least partially off the land," she reminded me.

"It is a little early for berries or fruit. On the seminary outing it was later in the year. There is obviously nothing to harvest here unless you wish to eat grass."

"We could grab a handful of that there watercress from the stream," Meg Hubbard suggested. We all went forward to the stream, where Meg lifted her skirt to form a basket and began snatching at little green leaves growing at the water's edge. When I saw which plants she was harvesting, I joined her and pointed out to Victoria that watercress made a dainty sandwich.

"There are tadpoles here!" Victoria exclaimed.

"By all means catch them if you feel like eating tadpoles."

"I'll go forward a ways and find a dry spot for to build a fire," Hubbard told us. "An arch like in the tall trees will keep us from lighting the entire forest. Lucky I kept the tinderbox dry. I know you would have warned me never to carry the tinderbox anywheres but next my heart wrapped up in oilskin if you'd thought of it, miss." His sly eyes glinted maliciously beneath his misshapen hat.

"Mind you use only dry twigs for the fire," I said, hoping to redeem my sagging reputation.

"You never mean water won't burn!" he grinned.

"And set up a tarpaulin in case the rain breaks in earnest."

He and Meg exchanged a snorting laugh, and he left. "You might want to pick a few mushrooms, miss," she said to conciliate me after her husband had left. "I'm sure you'll know which are safe to eat. Hubbard brought along a frying pan, so he can fry us up a batch."

"I didn't see any meadow mushrooms," I said. "They are perfectly safe."

"There's campies growing hereabouts."

"I expect you mean *agaricus campestris*, but it is very similar to the amanita, which is highly poisonous. We shan't risk it." She did not appear to know, and I did not inform her, that the *agaricus campestris* was, in fact, the meadow mushroom. I had not seen any, but no doubt Hubbard had.

"I can tell 'em apart right enough."

"I refuse to eat toadstools," Mrs. Irvine said grandly.

She found a fallen branch and, using it as a cane, hobbled to where Hubbard was building his fire. The rain did not increase, and the ground beneath the tall trees was dry. We filled our hands with watercress and went after her. Meg made darting trips to the fireside carrying assorted roots and leaves, which she assured us were entirely edible; in fact quite tasty. On her last trip her lifted skirt was heavy with mushrooms.

We had come out to rough it, and I insisted that Victoria and I have a part in feeding the fire and preparing tea. I was not at all confident in the edibility of the meatless ragout Meg was stirring up in a pot over the fire, but I was determined those questionable mushrooms would not pass Victoria's lips. When I saw Meg about to cut some of them into the ragout, I stopped her.

"Cook those separately, just in case. I don't advise you to eat them either, Meg. Mushrooms can be very dangerous."

"Not if you know what you're about," she sniffed. Her manner was unpleasantly saucy when Hubbard was nearby. She sliced the mushrooms into a frying pan with a spoonful of butter.

"They smell awfully good," Victoria said, sniffing the air.

I ignored her hint. "Let us wash out our eating vessels. They'll be filthy after falling in the bog."

We took them to the stream and swished them around to remove the muddy water. Of course, we had nothing to dry them with, but time would take care of that. Meg was about to pour the water on the tea when we got back.

"Are you sure that water had come to the boil?" I asked sharply, to show I was still in charge.

"It's just a-bubbling and a-hopping, miss," she assured me, and emptied it on the leaves.

"Damme if that rain isn't worsening," Mrs. Irvine said, pulling her pelisse about her.

As she spoke heavy drops began to plop from the trees. They fell with a hiss on the fire but did not quite extinguish it. Hubbard busied himself making a roof for the fire with assorted lids and logs.

"The fire needs air to burn," I told him.

"Aye, but she don't need water, do she? I'm leaving a draft for the air to seep in."

Wan tongues of orange continued to lick up through the charred logs and branches. Unappetizing chunks of root and unidentified leaves floated in our soup. The liquid was a mud brown color. Those mushrooms smelled better by the minute. I got the carving knife, wiped it on my skirt, hacked large pieces off a loaf of bread, and buttered them. Mrs. Irvine limped forward and grabbed one from my fingers. She wolfed it down as if she hadn't seen food in a week. I spread the watercress on the others and made them into sandwiches. They bore very little resemblance to the dainty sandwiches served in polite saloons, but I was looking forward with lively impatience to eating them.

138

"The fire's going out, Hubbard," his wife announced in portentous accents.

"Is the soup ready?"

She pulled out a piece of root, vaguely carrotlike in shape, but brownish in color, and tried it. "It's still tough," she replied.

"If you can get your teeth around it, we'd best eat it before she's cold."

The rain was falling faster now, wetting our hats and shoulders. There was more smoke than heat from the meager fire. The smoke kept the winged insects at bay, so we removed our veils. The picture before me fell into dreadfully sharp focus. I could see the grime on Victoria's face and gown. Beneath her sodden skirt, her lovely slippers were utterly destroyed. What would Marndale think when I brought her home in such a state? My mind wandered often to Marndale as I endured the vicissitudes of that wretched morning. My memories and thoughts for the future were of a piece with the present.

Mrs. Irvine, supported by the makeshift cane, stood as near the fire as the smoke allowed to dry her gown. Her face was pinched in pain. The Hubbards, who were so rough they wouldn't mind being caught in a war or a hurricane, were grinning fiendishly.

"How is your ankle, Mrs. Irvine?" I asked.

"It hurts, but you need not call off the expedition on my account. On horseback I can carry on."

"This is absurd. We'll just eat a bite and go back home."

A shiver convulsed Victoria, and she said, "That might be best. I fear these damp clothes might cause Mrs. Irvine a chill." It was Victoria I was more worried about. Mrs. Irvine's life at sea had inured her to hardship.

"We haven't even built our raft yet, let alone try her on the pond," Hubbard objected.

I turned to him. "Is the horse blanket—"

"Sopping wet," he answered cheerfully.

"Do you know of a cave nearby where we might eat our lunch?"

"Would I of made a fire in the open if I knew of a handy cave? There's none hereabouts. Ladle out the soup, Meg."

The Hubbards began their repast with a plate of steaming mushrooms, which they ate with the watercress sandwiches. While they enjoyed this treat, the rest of us sipped at the revolting soup. The leaves, though foul and bitter-tasting, were at least chewable. The roots defied us all, so we settled for tea and bread, with bits of the greenery adding color but very little taste. When there was as much rain as tea in our cups, I announced it was time to leave.

"Nay, it would be best to wait till the rain lets up," Hubbard said. "She won't last long. Why pelt onwards when the sun will be shining in no time? A little ways forward there's denser cover under the oaks and elms. Not a drop will come through to soak us. I'll just squelch the fire," he said, considering it settled.

"What fire?" Meg asked, but when he poured what remained of the water on it there was a fresh blast of smoke and ashes and some sizzling sound.

I didn't argue with him. He knew what he was about, and I did not. That was the sum and total of it. I could see Mrs. Irvine was tired. We all were. Our damp clothing clung to our backs, warning of possible chills to follow. A rest in a drier spot till the sun came out seemed a good idea. Belle was brought forward, and Mrs. Irvine was assisted aboard with much huffing and puffing by Hubbard and myself. While this was going forth, Meg and Victoria gathered up our utensils and loaded them into their bag. The bag was hung over the mount, and we forged ahead. The horse moved at an awkward gait, but I blamed it on the uneven ground and her heavy load.

As the omniscient Hubbard had prophesied, a dry place was near at hand. The low-hanging branches made it ineligible for a fire, but for a resting spot it was ideal. We propped Mrs. Irvine against a tree, I volunteered my pelisse to cover her, and she said, "Wake me when it's over," just before she closed her eyes with a luxurious sigh.

"I'm going to shoot me a brace of hare for dinner," Hubbard announced. He tossed his head in Meg's direction, and she hopped to his side like a dutiful wife. "Your papa won't mind, Lady Victoria?"

"Much you'd care if he did!" Meg snickered. He glared. She pulled in her chin and fell silent.

"You have my permission, Hubbard. You have been very helpful. I shall tell Papa you are an excellent guide," Lady Victoria replied.

He blushed with pleasure and I with shame. Were it not for Hubbard, we would have been in even worse straits than we were. Soon the woods reverberated with shots. No doubt every bullet brought the life of an unwitting hare to an end. The shots disturbed Mrs. Irvine at first, but as the Hubbards moved farther away the sounds became fainter, till at last they were mere echoes.

The young regain their strength with such ease. Soon Lady Victoria said, "What shall we do now, Jennie? Shall we walk through the woods a little and explore? You can describe and name all the wildflowers for me." She didn't mention my knowing anything about birds or wildlife.

My legs complained mightily when I stood up on them. A sting on my heel warned me of an incipient blister, but this was my opportunity to redeem myself, and I was happy enough to strike out. "Will we be able to find our way back?" she asked.

"That's what a compass is for." I drew out my

compass and explained its workings to her. It was a pleasant walk. I do know something about flowers even if you might not think it. I also explained to Victoria how one could judge the direction from the moss growing on the north side of the trees. We found mushrooms and pulled them apart to reveal the spores resting on the gills of the caps.

"They look like pepper," she said.

"They are like a plant's seeds. New mushrooms grow from these spores. A mushroom is an interesting thing, a parasite. It grows on dead vegetable matter. It springs up into showy prominence overnight, which is why parvenus are called mushrooms."

The sky cleared as we made a leisurely stroll, stopping often to examine some piece of nature. An echo of Hubbard's gun still occasionally rent the air. After an hour or so Victoria said, "I haven't heard Hubbard shooting for a while now. Perhaps we ought to go back."

"Yes, it is getting late, and we don't want to be wandering in the woods after dark. We'll go back and build a fire. And tomorrow we'll go on to the pond and build our raft."

We turned and began to retrace our steps. All the forest looked very much alike—trees and undergrowth. There was no stream to use as a landmark.

"Didn't we pass this way five minutes ago?" Victoria asked after awhile.

"All the trees look alike."

"I'm sure we passed this very spot. There, you see the picked flowers, where you were telling me about the stamens and pistils. Perhaps you ought to consult your compass, Jennie."

"Yes, this will be a good time for a practical lesson. We came northeast, so we must return southwest. This way," I said, setting off in the opposite direction to which we had been traveling. I was happy she had suggested the compass.

142

We proceeded swiftly now, with no stopping to examine nature. "We're here again!" Victoria exclaimed after another ten minutes. Sure enough, there were the wilted and disassembled wild flowers at our feet.

"This compass must not be working. The moss on the trees appears to be on the south side instead of the north. We'll follow the moss on the trees." I was beginning to feel a tremble of apprehension, though of course I did not let her see it.

After another ten minutes Jennie said, "There is moss on both sides of these trees, Jennie. What can account for it?"

"This must be a particularly damp spot."

"But how are we to know north from south?" she asked. Her eyes were large, and her face pale with anxiety.

"Now you must not panic," I said in a strained voice. "We'll shout for Hubbard. As we spent so long walking in circles, we cannot be far from Mrs. Irvine. He would be back by now." I raised my hands to my lips and shouted "Halloo!" four or five times. No answering call came to us but only the dead echo of my own shout.

"We are lost!" Victoria exclaimed, and burst into tears.

"Nonsense. I'll just give this compass a tap. The needle is probably sticking in the dampness." I tapped it and took the needle's word that our new direction was southwest. Victoria decided she felt safer holding onto my hand, which slowed our progress. It hardly mattered, as we were soon back at the dismembered wild flowers.

"We'll tie a ribbon on a tree every so often to alert us that we have passed that way before," I decided.

"Oh, you are so clever! I would never have thought of that."

I blushed at her praise. I felt like an utter incompetent as I ripped strips from my petticoat. Marking the trees had the effect of keeping us from going in circles, but alas, it did not lead us to our camp. It was growing dark under the spreading canopy of leaves. It was not the shadowy darkness of a cloudy sky but the denser darkness of the falling sun.

"We'll never get home!" Victoria said, her lower lip trembling.

"What nonsense!" I laughed gaily. "Your papa would eventually send out a search party if we failed to show up."

"Yes, but would they find us if it was nighttime?"

"We'd build a fire to show the way."

"I hope your flint box is dry."

I hadn't the heart to tell her I didn't have one. Before we were both reduced to tears there was a bellow in the distance. "Are you there, ladies?" It was Hubbard's raucous voice, and I was never so happy to hear a sound in my life. Celestial choirs of angels were nothing to the music of his uncouth bellow. I called back, and soon he came stampeding through the bush like a mad elephant. "Are you lost?" he grinned.

"Lost?" I laughed, as though I hadn't a notion what he was talking about. "Certainly not. We were just on our way back. How was the hunting, Hubbard?"

He was easily diverted to boast of his plunder. A brace of hare, three partridges, and a badger, which he told me Meg made into a dandy stew. I heartily wished she had made it at our camp, for I was ravenous for some hot food. We followed Hubbard for ten or fifteen minutes and eventually came out into the clearing where the others awaited us.

Mrs. Irvine was quiet, which alerted me to danger. She ought to have been ripping up at me for being away so long. "Let me have a look at that ankle," I said, lifting her skirt. It had puffed up like

144

an adder. An angry red hue showed through her silk stocking.

"You've sprained this. Shall I rip a strip from my petticoat and bandage it up?"

"I'll sacrifice mine. It serves me right for being fool enough to come along on this outing."

I let her do it, as I wasn't eager to reveal the condition of my own petticoat to Hubbard. She lifted her skirt and found the seam to get the rip started. She tore a strip six inches wide from it, and I bandaged her ankle. "I'm afraid we must cut this expedition short, Victoria," I said, with an air of reluctance. "This ankle requires a doctor's attention."

Victoria bore up uncommonly well to her disappointment. "Oh, yes, we must not take any chances," she agreed eagerly.

"Bring the mount here for Mrs. Irvine, Hubbard," I called, and he went to fetch the horse from where it was tethered, chewing the grass.

My heart fell to my feet when I noticed the poor animal was limping. "Oh dear! She's lamed," I said weakly.

A groan issued from Mrs. Irvine. "We'll never get home!"

"Aye, she's pulled a tendon. She might be able to hobble home herself, but she can't bear such a weight as Mrs. Irvine. No matter if we don't get home tonight," Hubbard said cheerfully. "The air's dried up. We have a bag full of flesh and fowl. The old malkin won't die of a little sprain, and a night under the open sky will be a rare treat, eh Miss Robsjohn?"

"Charming," I said, pinning him with a cold eye.

Chapter Fourteen

"Meg, pluck the partridges whilst I make us a fire," Hubbard ordered.

I went to help Mrs. Irvine, and under my breath I hissed, "I'll soon trim his wings. He is the sort of upstart who thirsts for authority."

"It takes one to know one," she shot back. Pain and discomfort were wearing her nerves thin.

Hubbard continued on in his upstart way. "I'll build our blaze alongside of where we had the fire at noon. Not the exact spot, for we dowsed it with water. Do you think you can handle things here till I get back, Miss Robsjohn? Now don't go wandering off, for I'm too busy to set off in search of you again."

I turned my steeliest schoolteacher's gaze on him. "You overreach your authority, Hubbard. You will do as I say, and I do not wish to have any birds plucked or cleaned in my presence." There was a deal more I wished to say to that creature. I wished to countermand every order he had given, but a fire did seem an excellent idea, and we could not build one here with the leaves practically touching our heads, nor could we walk far with a lame lady and mare.

He glanced warily at Lady Victoria. Seeing she did not support his rebellion, he reverted to the demeanor of a proper servant. "What do you suggest then, miss?" he asked.

"I suggest you build a fire and have a cup of tea before you return to Wycherly for assistance. There will be no need to bother Lord Marndale," I added hastily. "He is entertaining guests this evening. Just bring us a fresh mount for Mrs. Irvine and perhaps some food that we can eat as we walk home. Some fruit or buns."

"What about this here lame mount?" he asked. The mount whinnied piteously.

"I'll bandage Belle's ankle. She can make it home as long as she doesn't have to carry a load."

Afraid to take out his ill-humor on me, Hubbard said roughly to his wife, "What are you waiting for then? Gather up some twigs. I'll go fetch fresh water for the tea."

"I was just going to do that, Hubbard," she said meekly, and darted off.

After the Hubbards left I busied myself with Belle's ankle. Bandaging it required the entire remains of my petticoat, so I removed that article and set about tearing it into strips. Belle's ankle felt hot and was slightly swollen. I wet the bandages at the stream in hopes that the drying cotton would cool the sprain. Victoria helped me apply the bindings.

Now that our deliverance was in progress, I turned my fears to the future. What would Marndale say when he heard from Victoria—and worse, Hubbard—of this disastrous trip? To gauge Victoria's attitude, I said, "Well, I daresay this little out-

147

ing was different from what you thought, eh Victoria?"

Her smile was uncertain. "I expected there would be a few mishaps. It would have been very dull if nothing had happened, would it not? A pity we did not work in a lesson on the raft. But I think the trip has tested my mettle. Would you say I stood up to adversity as well as your former pupils, Jennie?"

Incredible as it seemed, she was still looking to me for approval. I was humbled by her anxious face waiting for my verdict. "You were splendid!" I said enthusiastically.

She gave a shy smile and held a fresh strip of cotton out to me. "When this job is done, I shall cut us some bread and butter it. You will want to help Mrs. Irvine hobble to the fire. She is a little out of curl, is she not? At her age she is probably not enjoying our outing as much as we are, but I think it was wonderful."

Tears stung my eyes so that I could not look at her for a moment. When I had blinked them away, I looked and saw that under her tousled curls and dirty face, she looked as happy as a cow in clover. I felt a perfect hypocrite to let her think I knew the first thing about roughing it in the bush, but with the meeting with Marndale still to come, I had no intention of declaring myself a dissembler.

"Do you really have to go to London, Jennie?" she asked.

"It is all arranged. I really must."

"Will you ask Papa to let me go to London with him? We could go on meeting there."

"I doubt he will heed my request."

"Oh, he will. He thinks very highly of you. What do you think of him?" she asked, and studied me with her big, bright eyes.

I cleared my throat nervously. "He seems a very good sort of father."

"Oh yes, the very best, but I didn't mean as a father. I meant as a husband. Now don't take a pet. I know you disapprove of his affair with Lady Pogue, but if he married you, that would soon come to an end."

"Good lord, Victoria. Where did you get the idea? Did he say something to you?"

"He told me to find myself a stepmother, and he would marry her and give me a brother. Well, I have found the stepmama I want. I know Papa must marry again because of needing an heir, and I want him to marry you."

I felt nearly as elated as if Marndale himself had offered for me. The idea pleased me greatly, but any marriage between us would be a marriage of convenience, and that was so utterly impossible that I could not encourage her in her hopes. The notion of a marriage of convenience itself did not repel me, but a marriage in which one party was very much in love and the other a philanderer promised no convenience to either party.

"There is nothing like that between us," I said firmly. "Your father will marry some great lady, Victoria. Someone from his own class. I am only a schoolmistress who had the good fortune to inherit a little money. A very little, in comparison with your father's fortune."

"Only a schoolmistress!" she laughed. "If you are only a schoolmistress, Wellington is only a soldier. Papa might marry a great lady, but on the other hand, he might marry someone like Rita Pogue. Do you think you could care for him? In time, I mean."

"He has many good qualities," I said vaguely.

Her satisfied little smile told me that she took it for approval in principle. Victoria went to cut the bread, and while I helped Mrs. Irvine toward the fire, my thoughts ventured into the future. Marndale's only interest in me was to provide his daughter a mother and himself a son. His first good impression of my mothering abilities would be sadly cured by this excursion. The trip revealed my lack of judgment. Then I thought of Lady Pogue, and my spirits sank. If he was to marry a nobody, it would at least be a beautiful nobody like Lady Pogue.

When a fire was raging and the kettle hanging on the makeshift hob, Hubbard, with great ceremony, handed his gun over to Meg to protect us and left at a trot for Wycherly. He disdained having his cup of tea before leaving. The civility with which he treated me suggested that he was as fearful of my report to Marndale on his behavior as I was of his. All was courteousness and tugging of the forelock and "Yes, Miss Robsjohn. Certainly, ma'am."

A sense of ease came over the party as we sat around the blazing fire with a hot mug of tea between our fingers and twilight turning the sky to a deep indigo blue. Birds left the trees in flocks for their final dizzying day's flight, filling the air with their sweet warble. As Hubbard was not there to correct me, I ventured an identification of a few of them. We watched and ate our bread and drank our tea as the birds went to their roost. The sky gradually darkened to black pierced with glittering stars, and silence fell.

When our rescuers arrived it seemed an intrusion. I could hardly believe Hubbard had had time to reach Wycherly yet, let alone return. Hubbard's head appeared first, with his misshapen hat pulled firmly over his brow. He was astride Silver Star. Before there was time to rise and greet our rescuer, another head and another horse appeared behind him.

"Papa!" Victoria squealed, and jumped up to greet him. "We didn't expect you to come. Jennie told you not to disturb Papa, Hubbard," she scolded.

"He insisted, miss. He was already at the stable saddling up to come after you."

Marndale just looked with his mouth ajar in shock. "Good God, you all look as if you've been mauled by tigers!" he exclaimed when he found his tongue.

A glance around the assembled company made me acutely aware of our appearance. I knew that I looked every bit as ragged as the others, with their hair all askew, their clothing in filthy tatters, and their faces dirty. Marndale had dismounted to pull Victoria into his arms. Over her head his eyes turned to me in a long, measuring gaze that took note of all my deshabille. The glow in those dark eyes did not suggest disapproval. Quite the contrary. A small smile hovered on his lips.

He detached himself from Victoria and came toward the fire. "I am sorry Hubbard took you from your party."

"I wasn't at the party. As he said, I was at the stable, saddling up. I expected you would have returned long ago when the rain continued for so long. I feared something had happened. It was half a relief when Hubbard came pelting in."

"It was not the rain that defeated us but Mrs. Irvine's accident. You are just in time for tea, Marndale," I said.

The leaping flames bathed him in a flickering, orange glow. The bizarre circumstances, the black night, and the gypsy fire, enhanced his appearance to something out of *Arabian Nights*. His face looked swarthy and romantic above his sparkling white shirt and evening jacket. He might have been a Gypsy prince surrounded by his tribe. Our gaze held for a long moment, then he turned to Mrs. Irvine.

"Are you in much pain, ma'am?" he asked.

"I feel as if I've done ten rounds with Gentleman Jackson. I might add that curst Belle of yours is no

151

gentleman, Marndale. She dumped me into the bog."

"She hasn't been ridden in a decade."

"Then we have not lamed one of your good mounts," I said with relief.

I thought he would be in a hurry to return to his party, but he sat down and had a cup of tea while we all regaled him with the details of our outing.

"Jennie was splendid, Papa," Victoria said. "And she said I was splendid, too. She taught me all about compasses and moss and flowers and pistils and stamens. I helped her bandage Belle's ankle, and we ate awful food—leaves and twigs and bark—because Belle fell into the stream and our food got all wet."

"A highly cultural expedition!" he laughed.

It was hard to go on being furious with him when he looked so handsome. Relief at seeing my disgrace being magically transformed into a victory softened my mood. But I remembered Lady Pogue and asked in a thin voice, "How is the party, Marndale?"

"Excellent."

"If we hurry, we can still have a few dances," Victoria said. Behind her father's back she flicked a quick glance at him, then at me, in a meaningful way. This is your chance, that look said.

Marndale saw my interest and said deliberately, "It will take you ladies three or four days to clean up."

This snub took the edge off my enthusiasm. To retaliate I said, "You must give my apologies to Lord Anselm. I had promised him a waltz."

"If we hurry, we can still have a few dances," Victoria repeated. She emptied the remains of her tea on the ground, and the Hubbards began gathering up the utensils.

"You have had enough excitement for one day," Marndale said firmly. "Jennie will want to see that

Mrs. Irvine is comfortably settled in for the night, and you will go straight to your bed, miss."

"I'm not a bit tired," she insisted, but he feigned deafness.

It was as good as a prohibition on our attending the dance. I turned my back on Marndale and began making a fuss over Mrs. Irvine. I found her makeshift cane, helped her up, and ordered Hubbard to bring the mount forward. It took the two gentlemen to get her into the saddle with Victoria holding Silver Star's head quiet.

Hubbard quenched the fire with water from the stream, and soon we were back on the trail homeward. Marndale offered me his mount, which I refused. Next he tried to get Victoria to take it, but if I was going to walk home, she was going to do likewise, so no one rode the beast. Marndale just walked along beside it.

Hubbard, who had the instincts of a homing pigeon, led the way followed by Meg and Belle with Mrs. Irvine behind them. Marndale walked his nag behind her with Victoria and me bringing up the rear. How Hubbard found a path through the pitch-black and perfectly impenetrable forest I do not know—or care. I never intended to willingly set foot in a forest again, even in daylight. Conversation was practically nonexistent as we forged our way onward. An occasional warning of a rock in the path or a wayward branch was about the sum of it. Once Marndale waited in a clearing for me and asked again if I was sure I did not wish to ride. Vickie left us alone, hoping for some romance to develop.

"You must be fagged," he said solicitously.

"I am not in the least tired, but you must not worry. I am not going to insist on attending your dance."

"You are perfectly welcome to attend, if you feel

up to it. Is it anticipation of that waltz with Anselm that overcomes your fatigue?"

"Very likely," I said offhandedly. I did not inquire if it was Lady Pogue's monopoly of his time that made him wish I were too fagged to dance.

"There is still the morning to see him," he said.

"True, but I hardly ever waltz in the morning. Especially when there is no music available. Let us go on, before we lose Hubbard."

He cocked his head and said playfully, "Would that be so bad? We have the formidable Miss Robsjohn to lead the way."

"You overestimate my abilities."

"Perhaps you underestimate them."

"Is there a point to this conversation, Marndale, other than delaying our return?"

He shrugged his shoulders. "Apparently not," he said curtly, and hurried off after the caravan.

As we continued I noticed my petticoat ribbons around two or three trees. They were not at all far from Wycherly. But then our entire excursion had not really taken us far as the crow flies. We must have made a crinkum-crankum trip into the woods, which made our trip seem longer than it was. Hubbard took us home in a straighter line.

While Hubbard took the other mounts to the stable, Mrs. Irvine rode Silver Star right up to the back door of the house. She slid off with no difficulty but needed assistance to walk. As soon as we entered the kitchen, Marndale asked Cook to send a girl upstairs to help Mrs. Irvine. He put his strong arm around her waist, she leaned her other arm on my shoulder, and in that fashion we got her up the servants' stairs and into her room. Victoria tagged along behind, still chattering and boasting about our outing.

"I'll send for a doctor," Marndale said when my

companion was laid out on the top of the counter-pane.

"I'll just take one of Jennie's headache powders, and if I still feel below the weather in the morning that will be time enough to call a sawbones. A twisted ankle isn't going to kill me. All I want now is to close my eyes and sleep," she said wearily. "I am even too tired to eat, though we haven't had a decent bite since we left." She did look burnt to the socket.

"I'll get my powders," I said, and left her.

Marndale was outside her door when I came out from delivering the medication. He looked a trifle sheepish, which made me wonder what had happened.

"Vickie has decided she will go below for a dance after all," he said. "As Mrs. Irvine plans to sleep immediately, perhaps you would like to join us. After you have made a toilette, I mean," he added, his eyes flickering over my condition.

Though I had insisted I was not tired, I did, in fact, feel as if I had run a steeplechase. The manner of the suggestion was more diffident than enthusiastic, but even if he had gone down on his knees, I would not have accepted an invitation by that time. "It will take me eons to get the dirt scraped from my body. Even my hair should be washed. You had best return to your guests, Marndale." It irked me greatly that he was happy with my answer. The satisfied lift of his lips revealed it.

"We'll have another dancing party before you leave," he said by way of compensation.

"That will be about five tomorrow morning, I assume? I have not had an opportunity to speak to you, but as we are home early from our outing, there is no reason Mrs. Irvine and I cannot leave tomorrow."

"Tomorrow! You were to stay till Monday!"

"No, we changed our minds."

"You cannot leave when Mrs. Irvine is ill."

"She is not ill. She has wrenched her ankle. Sitting in a well-sprung chaise will not punish it much."

"You cannot go tomorrow. The furniture is not even in the apartment yet. It is to be moved in over the weekend."

"The apartment?" I frowned, as if I scarcely knew what he was talking about. "Oh, we have decided against accepting your kind offer. We shall hire rooms somewhere. Mrs. Irvine feels it might look odd for me to be accepting favors from you."

"It is not a favor! It is payment for your looking after Vickie this past week."

"I no longer have to work for pay, sir. I thought I had made that perfectly clear."

I turned and strode angrily to my room. Marndale came hurrying after me, still arguing. "I don't understand!" he said in frustration. "What has happened? Why are you suddenly rushing off and refusing to use the apartment? I thought it was all settled."

With my hand on my doorknob I turned on him in a fury. "Nothing was settled! You think you have only to say the word and the whole world jumps to do your bidding. I never said I would take the apartment."

"But you asked when it would be ready."

That stymied me but not for long. "I was considering the matter. I have decided against it."

"But why?"

I did not wish to dredge up the whole unsavory business of Mrs. Pogue slipping into his room after the house was asleep, but at his badgering it came out. "Because I have my reputation to consider, sir. I was not aware when I agreed to stay here that you were in the habit of having your mistress un-

156

der your own roof. What will anyone think to hear that I am making a prolonged visit to Wycherly and especially that I have accepted an apartment in London from you?"

He looked perfectly blank. *"Mistress?"* he exclaimed.

"You dissemble uncommonly well, Marndale. At least you take pains to conceal that Lady Pogue joins you after the rest of us are asleep."

"I don't know what you're talking about."

"Your discretion is not necessary with me. I know, and your daughter knows, what is going on here. I should think you might wait till you are in London at least."

His brows drew together in a sharp frown. "What do you mean, my daughter knows? What have you been telling her?"

"Nothing. It was she who informed me of the relationship."

"This is impossible," he said brusquely.

"Is it? Then no doubt you will straighten Victoria out."

"You may be very sure I will!" he growled, and went stalking off in the direction of Victoria's room.

My knees felt about as firm as water and my heart was hammering in my throat, but I managed to get the door open and went into my room.

Chapter Fifteen

My room was like a mausoleum. All was silent blackness around me, but as my eyes adjusted I discerned a watery moonbeam piercing the window. By its ghostly glimmer the chamber took shape. There was a pale rectangle of mirror at my toilette table, a larger, higher rectangle of canopied bed. Gradually the smaller furnishings took form as I stood, drawing in the sweet scent of flowers from the roses on my desk. By the moon's eerie illumination I found the tinderbox and lit one lamp, then fell down on the bed in a state of disorientation.

Why had I not held my wretched tongue? Now Marndale would go badgering Victoria, and she would hate me, too, for betraying her confidence regarding the coal scuttle in Lady Pogue's bed. But really it was infamous of him to deny it when there was hard, tangible evidence of what was going on. It seemed a gentleman was permitted to lie in defense of a lady's reputation.

Time was irrelevant. I lay, not so much thinking as letting my mind drift where it would. Some time later the idea came to me that life must go on. I realized that part of the pain inside me was due to hunger, and I crawled up from the bed to ring for a tray. I caught a glance of myself in the mirror and saw that bathing must take precedence even over eating. I did indeed look as if I had been battling wild animals. My Titian hair was dulled with dust. Bits of twig and dry leaves clung to it. Dogs who have been rolling in the muck look as I looked. My face and gown suggested I had been dragged through the woods, not walked. Every square inch of me bore some disgusting filth from the bog.

I rang for a servant and asked for a tub of hot water to be followed by food. Any kind of food. I would have eaten the pig's breakfast by that time. I peeled off my clothes and threw them into the wastebasket—stockings, shoes and all. They were beyond redeeming. Till the water came I wrapped myself in a blanket and sat, shivering. It was not cold, but my thoughts sent trembles down my spine. The morning, with the Eldons and Lady Pogue, could not possibly be anything but ignominiously embarrassing. I would not leave my room till I learned the other guests had departed.

Three girls brought the tub and water and poured my bath. The tub was a pretty white enamelled affair trimmed with pink flowers. I washed my hair in my china basin then gratefully sank into the warm tub and let the water ease the aches from my poor battered body and spirit. The future seemed endurable with the warm water lapping over me. I just lay my head back against the tub and closed my eyes.

When the water began to cool down I scrubbed myself all over and got out, wrapping myself in a soft towel. I pulled on my nightdress, wrapped my peacock peignoir around me, and rang to have the tub exchanged for a tray. After I had towelled my hair and combed it I went down to visit Mrs. Irvine till my dinner arrived. The servants had helped her to wash and change into her nightclothes. She was just on the verge of sleep, so I left her.

I rather thought I might have an incendiary visit from Victoria after her father spoke to her, but she didn't come. She was disgusted with me then. She had accepted my mismanagement of the excursion, but betraying her to her father had finally turned her against me.

"Has Lady Victoria gone downstairs yet?" I asked the girl who brought my tray.

"She changed her mind, Miss Robsjohn. She just went to bed—with a flea in her ear, I believe," the girl said, holding back a titter. "I could hear them at it, the pair of them, when I brought up your tub. His lordship—"

I gave her a blighting look to show her I was not interested in gossip. "That will be all, thank you," I said.

Once I held the tasty tray in my hands I realized how impossible it would be to eat. The food looked delicious. It was from the supper table Victoria and Cook had devised to feed the dance party, but neither ham nor fowl, lobster nor even cream chantilly appealed to me. I sat at the desk and nibbled on a leg of chicken and a piece of bread, as I did not wish to return the tray untouched.

I was sitting, looking at a dish of lobster and thinking, when a knock at the door startled me out of my reverie. I moved quietly to the door and listened. Victoria or Marndale? If it was Victoria, I wished to speak to her, but I really could not face her father again that night. I waited a moment, undecided.

"Jennie, are you there?"

It was Marndale's voice. I stood silent, frozen to the spot. He tapped again, more loudly. "Jennie?"

I didn't move. I hardly dared to breathe. Soon I heard his footsteps recede down the hallway. Of course, I wondered what he wanted, but I did not regret my behavior. Even when I realized he must have seen the light beneath my door and knew I was awake, I wasn't sorry. I extinguished the lamps and got into bed. Through the embracing silence soft echoes from the ballroom wafted up the stairs. I mentally danced a quadrille with Marndale; then the waltz music began. That was to have been Anselm's dance, but in my mind it was Marndale whose arms were around me, his dark eyes that gazed lovingly into mine. He was probably dancing with Lady Pogue. I turned over angrily. Three waltzes and a cotillion later, I slept. I didn't hear the houseguests coming upstairs.

I was awakened in the morning by golden sunlight slanting through the window. I had forgotten to draw the draperies. It looked a fine day for my trip to London. I dressed in my green travelling suit and arranged my hair carefully. Its washing left it bright as a new penny and bouncing with curls. When I was ready I did not descend below but rang for a tray. I held to my decision not to go below till the guests had left. While waiting for my breakfast I began to sort out my gowns for packing. This was my occupation when the tap came at the door.

"Come in," I called, thinking it might be Victoria.

The door opened, and Lord Marndale stepped in, carefully leaving the door open behind him for propriety's sake. He saw the gowns on the bed, and a frown drew his brows together.

"You might be interested to know Mrs. Irvine is in no condition to travel," he said curtly. That was his greeting.

"Nonsense!"

"The doctor has just left her. Her ankle is very sore, and her shoulder is wrenched as well."

"We'll set a slow pace. London is not that far away."

A dangerous sparkle flashed in his eyes. "Have you no consideration for anyone but yourself! You cannot drag that poor woman all the way to London, to arrive half dead with no home to take her to."

In my excitement I had forgotten all about returning to Bath. "We shall take rooms at an hotel till we find something. You must not trouble yourself with our welfare, Lord Marndale. It is really none of your concern."

"I suppose it is not my concern that you filled Victoria's head with malicious stories about my carrying on with Lady Pogue either," he retorted. "You actually taught my daughter to set a trap to catch me, as if I were a common felon. It is unconscionable what you have done."

I regretted that open door, for his voice was rising to a high pitch. "I did nothing of the sort," I said in a lower but equally angry tone. "The idea came from my chaperone, and Lady Victoria executed the scheme without informing us. As you think me capable of such behavior, however, I should think you would be happy to see me leave as soon as possible."

"Not like this. We have to talk, to straighten this mess out. Lady Pogue did not visit me, either the night before last or any other time."

I gave him a withering look. "Just as you say, Marndale. I have heard you, and so will the rest of the house if you don't stop shouting."

He ignored my hint and my worried glance at that open doorway. "I am telling the truth. I think

I know what blinds you to what has *really* been going on."

I was hard put to find the reason for his words and the meaningful stare that accompanied them. "I'm afraid I don't understand you."

"Think about it."

I thought about it without gaining any enlightenment whatsoever. "Perhaps Lady Pogue sleeps curled up in a tight ball so that her feet did not encounter the coal scuttle," I said with a careless shrug.

"That is not the explanation that occurred to me."

"No sane explanation occurs to me. If you would cease talking in riddles and tell me what you mean—"

A blaze of frustration lit his eyes and an angry flush colored his cheeks. "You know I can't do that."

"I don't see why the devil not."

His frustration did not decrease. He stiffened up and said curtly, "The guests are preparing to leave. No doubt you would like to go below and speak to Anselm before he goes."

"No, I shall see him in London."

He reefed his hands through his hair. "I don't understand what you are about. Lady Pogue is nothing to me. She was not invited here for *my* amusement. No slur can possibly attach to your remaining to complete your visit. Indeed the whiff of impropriety only arises at your hurried departure."

I lifted my chin and said, "Would you be kind enough to ask the servants to let me know when the guests are gone?"

He clenched his lips, shook his head in confusion, and finally said, "Very well, if that is what you really want."

"I wouldn't ask you to do it if I didn't want it."

Yesterday Victoria had spoken of the Eldons and Bathursts leaving today. I had thought at the time that Lady Pogue and Anselm were to remain, but Marndale had not mentioned any change of plans. If it was his intention to make me an offer, he would not want his mistress in the house, however, so that really meant nothing. And the only reason in the world he would be offering for me instead of her was that Victoria did not like Lady Pogue. The maid arrived with my tray, subjected us to a mute, goggling examination, and went to place the tray on the desk. Marndale scowled and left at a stiff-legged, angry gait.

I noticed the servant's eyes had settled on the wastebasket holding my soiled gown. "Shall I empty that for you, miss?"

"The upstairs maid will do it, but you can remove last night's tray."

"Are you casting that there gown aside, miss?" she asked hungrily.

I understood what she was about then and said, "Yes; perhaps you would like to take it to use as rags."

Her poor, dull eyes lit up like a lantern. "Rags? I'll have me a new Sunday gown from that."

She snatched up the dust basket, put the supper tray atop it, and left, smiling as if she had won the lottery. I could not feel too sorry for myself when there were such unfortunate creatures in the world. I sat down and began my breakfast. I was interrupted by another tap on the door. Marndale was the first thought that flew into my head, but it was Victoria who came in without waiting for me to answer.

She was wreathed in smiles, and I smiled, too, for I was very happy that we were to part as friends. "Good morning, Victoria. You're up early," I said.

"Early? It's ten o'clock. The guests are preparing to leave."

"I know they are. I should be packing, too."

She glanced at the gowns tumbled out on the bed. "You're not leaving!"

"You knew I was to leave as soon as the expedition was over."

"You must stay. I was wrong about Lady Pogue, Jennie. Papa didn't know what I was talking about when I told him about the coal scuttle. He was furious with me and wouldn't let me go to the dance—not that I cared about that. There was no one there but old men anyway. I think it must have been Anselm she visited. Are you very disappointed?" I received a shaft from those peculiarly mature eyes.

Anselm? Although Marndale had mentioned him a few times, that long-chinned gentleman featured so little in my thoughts that I had not realized what Marndale was implying. His foolish honor prevented him from accusing Anselm outright of carrying on with that pretty trollop of a Rita Pogue, but that was his meaning. And he thought that I would be crushed at the knowledge. The idiot thought I was in love with Lord Anselm. He must think me uncommonly fond of chins.

I was thrilled to death to learn the truth. "Why should I be disappointed?" I asked, weak with relief.

"Papa thinks you like him since you're always talking to him and about him."

"I know his sister. We just talk about the seminary," I explained.

"Perhaps Anselm hopes you would be her companion."

This humiliating idea had the whiff of truth to it. He did speak of Lady Mary a good deal. I recalled, too, that Lady Pogue had said she did not care to chaperone a grown lady as it would put her amongst the matrons. Was it Lady Mary she meant and not Victoria? Marndale said he had not invited Lady Pogue for his own amusement. He had done it for Anselm's benefit.

"You wouldn't be Lady Mary's companion when you refuse to be mine, would you?" Victoria asked, ready to take offense.

"Certainly not. If I were to act as companion for any young lady, Victoria, it would be you. But I do not have to work, you know. It would be selfish to take work away from some lady who needs a position."

"It wouldn't be selfish to marry Papa," she said with an arch smile. Then she danced out the door, and I was left behind with my head in a whirl.

And it remained in a whirl for the rest of the morning. Lady Bathurst dropped in to make her adieux. "Miss Robsjohn," she smiled. "What a pity you missed the party last night. I could not leave without taking my leave of you and Mrs. Irvine. You must not think because I left the saloon with Lady Eldon the other night that I preferred her company. My dear, a dead bore! I was longing for more of your companion's naughty chatter. My duty, however, was to keep Elizabeth in good humor. Bathurst and Marndale are trying to bend Eldon's ear in some political monkey business or other. He pays heed to his lady's opinions. It would not do to offend her at such a delicate time. What we political wives have to put up with!"

"How very kind of you to call," I said, flushed with pleasure. Lady Bathurst was top of the trees, a real lady, as opposed to the cit, Lady Eldon.

"Let me know when you reach London, and we shall get together to talk over this horrid visit. What a dull scald it has been, but at least Marndale sets a good table. Oh, by the by, Lady Eldon said to say good-bye for her, too. La Pogue will pay her own respects."

Lady Pogue did as threatened. She came waltzing in, looking as beautiful as ever. "You missed a famous party, Miss Robsjohn," she said. "Dick was so disappointed that you could not make it."

"But then he had you to console him," I smiled knowingly.

"Ah, you have found us out. I told him he wasted his time, trying to persuade you by flirting."

"Persuade me to act as companion to Lady Mary, you mean?" I wanted to get it all perfectly clear.

"It would not have been at all unpleasant. But then I told him, why should Miss Robsjohn work when she is so terribly pretty and has a little fortune? And if she was to settle for a gentleman's country estate for the job, why leave Wycherly? He thought Lady Mary would be an inducement. That cow-eyed miss! Men! They never understand anything," she laughed. "I'll call after you are settled in London. We'll find you a parti, never fear. I was afraid you might steal Dick from me," she added.

I made some vague reply. "Oh, by the by," she said just as she was leaving. "What has got Marndale in a pet? He was looking daggers at Dick and me over breakfast. I hope Dick has not made a mess of whatever it is he's doing for Marndale. He hopes for a cabinet post if the Whigs ever win an election."

"Actually, I think Marndale was angry with me."

She examined me with the liveliest curiosity. "You are shooting just a little high, I think, but one never knows. You have certainly got Vickie on your side. She has been singing your praises till we were all wishing we had gone on that delightful excursion. Good luck!" She fluttered a farewell and left.

I finally got down the hallway to see Mrs. Irvine. She was sitting up and looked in fighting trim.

"I hear you are not recovered," I said. By this time I was eager to find her too ill to travel.

"I never felt better. There was no need to send for

a sawbones. Marndale did it without asking me. The swelling in my ankle has begun to go down already."

"But your shoulder—"

She made a circling motion with her shoulder. "It is a little stiff. Getting up and about will cure it faster than lying here all day, staring at the ceiling. Just tell me when you wish to leave, and I shall be ready."

"There is no hurry. Why don't you just rest for one more day? We shouldn't travel on a Sunday in any case."

"Those rigid rules don't apply outside of Bath. The others are all leaving."

"We shall leave on Monday, Mrs. Irvine."

She crossed her arms and glowered. "I know when I am being conned. I'll have the truth, if you please. What is afoot, Jennie?"

"You look pale, Mrs. Irvine."

"Of course I look pale, ninny. I have not put on my rouge yet."

Marndale appeared at the door and finding it open stepped in. "Anselm is downstairs. He would like a word with you before he leaves, Jennie." His face was grave and pale.

Knowing what that word would be, I said, "Pray say good-bye for me. I cannot go now. I'm busy."

A travesty of a smile appeared on his ravaged countenance. "I'll tell him," he said, and left with alacrity to do it.

I deduced from his odd behavior that he feared Anselm might offer for me. How he could think such a thing after the affair of the coal scuttle, I don't know, but nothing else could account for his expression. I suppose it is not unknown for a man to propose to a lady behind his mistress' back.

A minute later Marndale was back at the door, carrying a note. With a house full of servants it was odd he performed these errands himself. "I am to await a reply," he said, handing it to me.

He watched as I unfolded the sheet. The note had obviously been written in haste, for it was not at all diplomatic. It said: "Dear Miss Robsjohn: Would you consider undertaking the care of Lady Mary at Levington Hall in Kent (close to London!)? Name your price! Hopefully, Anselm."

I could choke down my rage as the message was no surprise. With Marndale's dark eyes studying me, I even allowed a smile to grace my lips.

"I can take a verbal reply," Marndale suggested. His face was alive with curiosity.

To tease him I insisted on writing my answer. The only sound in the room was the scratching of the pen on paper. I was aware of a yawning silence behind me, and glancing over my shoulder, I saw that Marndale was watching me as a cat watches a mouse hole—with total absorption. Mrs. Irvine was studying him in the same intent manner. I just jotted a few words on the bottom of Anselm's note. "Sorry. I have other plans, but can recommend Miss Lydia Hopkins, from the seminary at Bath, for the job. J. Robsjohn."

I handed it to Marndale. "So kind of you," I smiled.

After he left Mrs. Irvine demanded, "What was that all about? Was it an offer from Anselm?"

"Yes, an offer to mind his sister, but you are not to tell Marndale so."

"What should I say if he asks?"

"That we did not discuss the matter. Now, can I get you something to drink? A book, perhaps."

"A servant to help me pack," she suggested.

"I am afraid you cannot recover just yet, Mrs. Irvine."

"If I must lie about all day, then I must have my rouge pot."

"Oh no! Invalids must be pale."

"Paleness does not afflict sly schemers, I see. Your rosy cheeks betray you, Jennie. If I am to lie

169

on my back like an overturned beetle, at least bring me my netting basket. And a fresh pot of tea."

"Certainly, but you must not get out of bed till I say so."

"What determines your saying so?"

"The offer Marndale is about to make. If it is like Anselm's, then you may recover by noon and let me be ill. If it is different—"

"So that's how it is. You are a pea goose if you hope to get an offer of marriage from a marquess. Rich noblemen don't marry schoolteachers, no matter how many airs the ladies give themselves. You never learn from your mistakes. You have just this minute learned what Anselm wanted from you, with all his smirking and compliments."

"You must have noticed, Mrs. Irvine. Marndale was not smirking. Quite the contrary."

After a frowning pause she acceded to my view. "I wondered when he was scooting in and out like a lackey with those notes. . . . He *did* look miserable enough to be trying to crank himself up to the sticking point."

"Well put." I smiled benignly and went in search of her netting basket and to order her tea.

I pondered how so many misunderstandings had arisen. Marndale thinking I cared for Anselm—perhaps we had behaved as old friends. Why had Lady Pogue been at such pains to initiate me into the rites of landing a London beau and assured me it would be easy to accomplish? Was it because she feared I might prove competition with Anselm if I went to Levington Hall? There were still a few misapprehensions to be cleared up, and I was eager to begin.

Chapter Sixteen

The delicate chore now facing me was to inform Lord Marndale that Mrs. Irvine was too worn to travel without revealing any weakness in my own position. The very real possibility still existed that Marndale wanted no more from me than a companion for his daughter. Anselm hoped to recruit me by flirting, why not Marndale? Contrary to what my companion thought, I was alive to that degrading possibility. An offer from his daughter hardly constituted a proposal of marriage or even the likelihood of one. My plan was to carry on my normal occupations with Victoria as if nothing unusual had occurred. Marndale had until Monday to speak to me, one way or the other.

He heard of my decision to remain through Victoria, who had come to visit Mrs. Irvine when I brought the netting box.

"I am so glad you are to stay, at least till Monday," Victoria said.

"Yes, indeed. We shall let you drive on the main highway today, Victoria. And I must drop

in on the Munsons to say good-bye to Peter and
Paul."

"That would be the twins you spoke of?" Mrs.
Irvine asked, pulling the needle from her netting.
I nodded. "You know what causes twins, of course?"
I feared for what lewd notion was to follow, and she
rushed on with Victoria hanging on every word.
"When a man and woman—"

"That's enough, Mrs. Irvine!"

"But I would love for Papa to have twins!"

"Then Mrs. Irvine may speak to your papa."

"Figure it out for yourself," Mrs. Irvine said with
a wink. "What makes one baby if done once will
make two if done twice on the same occasion."

"Let's go for our drive now, Victoria."

Victoria was so enthralled with this misguided
lesson in reproduction that she sat unmoved by an
invitation to her favorite pastime. "And for trip-
lets, three times," she said, nodding sagely. "Good
gracious, the Fortescues have quadruplets!"

"He must be some stallion!" Mrs. Irvine exclaimed, vastly impressed.

I got a hand on Victoria and dragged her from
the room by main force. "You won't mention this
to your papa, Victoria," I said.

"I expect he already knows."

"You must not listen to the rambling of ignorant—of superstitious—of simple—"

"Perhaps you're right. Odd that Mrs. Irvine has
no children. Surely she and her husband must
have—"

"It was the rocking of the ships that caused her
miscarriages," I said curtly. "Now go and get your
bonnet and pelisse."

I darted swiftly to my room and grabbed my bonnet, which gave me a few minutes to loiter in the
hallway below, hoping for a sight of Marndale. He
either heard my noisy descent—I called rather

loudly for the butler to have the carriage brought around—or he espied me from his office. He came strolling out with an unwonted air of distraction and pretended to be surprised to see me.

"Ah, Jennie. So you have taken my advice and decided to remain a few days."

"Yes, I fear Mrs. Irvine is really not stout enough to travel till Monday. Monday morning early we shall leave, as planned," I added, to let him know how long he had to speak.

"It is for the best. No point in jostling her in her condition."

"The ankle is improving. I hadn't realized she gave her shoulder such a wrench. I daresay it happened when Belle rolled her over in the bog."

"A fall can be a nasty thing."

"A bog is soft falling, if messy. It would have been worse on hard ground."

"Oh, infinitely! I once gave my ankle such a turn I couldn't walk for a fortnight. Just at a very busy time, too, of course. It's always the way."

The very banality of our conversation told me nothing was to come of it. It sounded dreadfully as though I had been imagining things. Victoria came pelting down before anything more could be said.

"Off for your driving lesson, eh?" her father said in that hearty way that wishes to confer an air of interest where none exists.

"On the main highway today, Papa," she boasted.

"Then I shall be sure to stay off the roads. Ha ha." Victoria pouted playfully. I looked bored, and he continued, "What have you ladies planned for this afternoon?"

"We are going to see the Munson twins before Jennie leaves," Victoria said.

He looked at me over her head. It was an interested, impatient look. "See if the rig is at the door, Vickie," he said.

We all knew the butler would tell us when it arrived, but none of us said so. She left, and Marndale continued. "I gave Anselm your message. He appeared disappointed at your reply. I take it it was a refusal?"

"Yes."

"Ah." He studied me closely, wanting to ask for more details but prevented by good manners.

"It's here, Jennie!" Victoria called from the doorway.

"Wish us well," I said, and turned to leave.

His hand reached out and grasped my wrist. "Jennie, before you go . . . there is something . . ." Surely I was not mistaking the cause of that glow in his eyes.

"Come on," Victoria called impatiently.

He gave her a dark look and said to me, "We'll talk when you return." I had to leave with that tantalizing promise preying on my mind.

You may imagine how little attention was paid to Victoria's driving. She must have acquitted herself reasonably well, for we returned without having been capsized. I could not recall any close shaves either.

"Excellent!" I complimented when we reached Wycherly. My mind flew in the door before me, anticipating the pending visit with Marndale. I knew he had been anticipating it, too, for he stuck his head out his office door the moment we entered. Victoria danced forward, and I followed.

"I did splendidly, Papa. Didn't I, Jennie? Now the carriage is mine, and I shall have it painted green."

He made a great fuss over her. "Well done! No white ponies, mind, but I might find you your own set of matched bays or grays if you would like."

"Do you think cream ponies pretentious, Papa?

Lady Pogue tells me cream ponies from the Prince Regent's stud are all the crack."

"We shall see," he said, and she was content with that. She darted upstairs to relay her success to Mrs. Irvine, and Marndale invited me into his office.

We stood facing each other with such a weight of anticipation in the air that it was nearly palpable. "So you have rejected Anselm's offer," he said, eying me warily, as if I might try to bite him.

"Yes." I waited to be offered a seat, but he either forgot or preferred to remain standing.

"I daresay the fact that he has a grown sister had something to do with your decision?"

This revealed that he believed the offer to have been for marriage. I read in it also some apprehension that his having a grown daughter might make me reject him. "It was the only reason I received the offer," I replied, true in word if not spirit.

"I shouldn't think that the *only* reason."

"You are free to think what you like. I happen to know that this was his reason."

"He is a demmed awkward fellow if he told you so." He smiled uneasily.

I had had enough of running around in circles. "What was it you wished to talk about, Marndale?" I asked bluntly.

"I have been thinking about Victoria. She is very keen to accompany me to London."

"Yes, she mentioned it to me, the possibility of our continuing to see each other." I said not a word about returning to Bath.

"The problem is, London without a truly excellent companion offers such a world of mischief for a lively girl like Vickie. My idea was that you and Mrs. Irvine might live at my London house with us instead of taking the apartment on Audley Street."

My heart sank like an anchor into the cold sea.

175

So this was all he wanted—a companion for Victoria. He had never said otherwise. I had once again let optimism run away with common sense. "I'm not interested. Thank you for the offer."

"There would be collateral benefits," he continued eagerly. "Superior company, a much better house than the Audley Street apartment, the use of my theater box, carriages, horses. You would be a guest, not an employee, though I would be happy to pay you—" He came to an embarrassed halt. I think he regretted his last words.

"I believe I have made clear I am not interested in employment, Marndale."

He shuffled his feet and said, "Victoria has never been so happy and well behaved as she has with you. I would do *anything* to convince you to remain with us. Is there any way I can convince you?" A pregnant pause, during which he gulped, then said warily, "Marriage—"

The word hung like a rotten apple on the bough. Even Eve would not be tempted by this inedible fruit. I spoke roughly to hide my disappointment. "You are even more generous than Lord Anselm. He gave me carte blanche to name my own price in his offer to mind Lady Mary, but I doubt he included marriage."

"What?"

"He offered me the position of minding Lady Mary at Levington Hall."

"Good God!"

"I refused, as I intend to refuse all such offers, even if they include a titular marriage. You must excuse me now. I have to see Mrs. Irvine. I shall be taking lunch with her in her room. Good day, Lord Marndale. Sorry I couldn't accommodate you."

I dashed upstairs, blinded by unshed tears of shame and sorrow, and went straight to my own room. I couldn't face anyone yet, not even Mrs. Irvine. What I really wanted to do was to leave Wycherly at once, but I was ashamed to suddenly declare Mrs. Irvine miraculously recovered. There was nothing for it but to camp out in her room till Monday morning when we could leave as planned.

As soon as I could lift up my head I began to execute this plan. I played with my luncheon in Mrs. Irvine's room, moving around a piece of beefsteak with a fork and sighing. Over the afternoon we had a raft of visitors. Every time I heard a footfall my heart went into palpitations, always in vain. Our callers were not such prestigious ones as the morning had brought to my bedchamber, but only Victoria and servants. Victoria came up after lunch and seldom left the room, which made any meaningful conversation difficult, though I had already confessed my shame to Mrs. Irvine and been informed with ill-concealed satisfaction five or six times that she had told me so.

Meg Hubbard came crashing in, fire in her eyes. Her excuse was to bring wine, which she hurled onto the bedside table with a clatter. "That was a mighty fine dress you gave Sal, Miss Robsjohn," she said angrily. "A pity it don't fit her wide hips. It would have fitted me just right."

I saw my meager charity had caused havoc below and quickly decided which other gown I could do without. "I thought you might prefer a muslin gown, Meg, with summer coming on."

"You never mean that dandy blue-sprigged one you've been a wearing?"

Indeed I did not! "No, a yellow-sprigged one, to match your hair."

"Lud, wait till Hubbard hears this." She ran off, smiling from ear to ear.

Hubbard's excuse to come begging was to present me with a wing from a partridge he had shot. "You'll find it dandy for dusting off the lids of books," he assured me. "You just slide her along the tops of the books on the shelf." It would have to be a very narrow book shelf. A goose wing was more commonly used.

"Thank you, Hubbard." I ransacked my mind for what I could give him. A lady's belongings would be of no use to this outdoorsman, and I settled on money. A crown seemed to satisfy him. I deduced that I should have tipped the servants who accompanied us on our excursion.

Cook came huffing upstairs in person, not to beg but to ask what she might cook to tempt the invalid. She said to me, "His lordship wants to know if you'll be eating dinner at the table, Miss Robsjohn."

"No, I shall bear Mrs. Irvine company in her room."

"As you wish, but I'm making up a dandy ragout."

"It can be brought upstairs, can it not?"

"It won't be hot when it reaches you. Not with the servants all fighting and flipping coins for the honor of delivering to this room." She shook her head and left.

My largesse to the servants appeared to be gaining mythical proportions belowstairs. Victoria had been studying me as if I were some rara avis she was unlikely to see again in her lifetime. "We could serve Mrs. Irvine's dinner early," she suggested. "You could sit with her while she eats then come downstairs to dine with me and Papa."

"And leave her alone? That would be uncharitable."

"I wouldn't mind a little of my own company," Mrs. Irvine said testily. "In fact, I'd like a nap. Run along, Jennie."

"Very well. I could do with a nap myself, but I shall join you for dinner and the evening."

178

Victoria and I left. "I'm going to Munsons'," she said. "I'll say your good-byes for you."

I knew what was expected of a legend and gave her a coin to give Mrs. Munson for Paul. From my bedroom window I gazed out on the terraced gardens. It was a beautiful day. One of those marvelous spring days when some green enchantment hangs on the air. Sunlight gleamed on Capability Brown's serpentine stream, luring me outdoors. Victoria had left, and it was unlikely that Marndale would be wandering in the garden. I picked up my parasol and ran down the servants' stairs. Cook's helper looked hopefully at my parasol, but I held on to it and got outdoors before having to dispense any more reluctant charity.

To insure privacy I hurried away from the house. The roses were in bloom, filling the eye with beauty and the air with perfume, but I wanted a wilder, more romantic ambience for my repining. I strolled along the edge of the serpentine, determined to trace it to its natural source, before Brown had got at it with his artistic clumps of three birches and flowering shrubs.

I came at last to a wilderness that perhaps indicated the edge of Marndale's domain or at least of his cultivated park. The banks of the stream were higher and more sharply inclined. On top of the slope a wall of intertwining camellias grew as tall as trees. The jungle of branches and dark green leaves was bereft of blossoms in this season save for one lone white flower that had bloomed late. I wanted to pick it, but it was too high.

I found a rock and sat down, gazing at the flowing stream below, edged in swaying sedge with a carpet of bog myrtle climbing up the embankment. Wild flowers dotted the meadow on the other side. Campion, buttercups, daisies, and ragged robin bathed in the golden sunlight. It was a scene to clutch at the heartstrings and make a lady wish she could live forever amidst such beauty. But spring would pass, and the flowers would die. The grass would turn brown and sere, the blue skies fade to lead, and the golden sunlight hide behind fog.

These were my thoughts when I heard the clatter of hooves. Looking up, I saw in the distance a mounted rider cantering through the meadow, advancing toward me. As I watched the rider took the form of a gentleman in a curled beaver and a blue coat. At closer range I saw the gentleman was Lord Marndale. I could either take to my heels and run, like a widgeon, or sit and hope he passed with no more than a tip of his hat.

His mount slowed when he reached the stream and picked its way daintily across not two yards from me. A word at least was required.

"A lovely day for a ride, Marndale," I said.

"You said you were going to the Munsons'," he replied.

He was coming from that general direction. On horseback he did not have to stick to the roads. I felt in my bones he had been there looking for me.

"I changed my mind. I was with Mrs. Irvine, but she is having a nap."

He drew his gelding to a stop and dismounted. It was impossible to read his mood. He looked fairly grumpy. "Then we can have our talk now," he said, turning from me to tie his mount to a nearby tree.

"We've already had it. My answer is no."

He looked over his shoulder at me. His dark eyes wore a glint of mischief or danger—or perhaps something else. "You haven't heard my question yet."

Chapter Seventeen

It was a large, low, table-like rock that I sat on. Marndale came forward and sat beside me. His longer legs had some difficulty arranging themselves. "I've just been to the Munsons'," he said.

"Very likely you met Victoria there."

"Yes. She said you were having a nap." He moved his legs about, trying to get comfortable.

"How are the twins?"

"Paul has a touch of colic."

"Nothing serious, I hope?" It was beginning to look like another of those pointless conversations leading nowhere. Next we would be saying what a beautiful day it was.

"Mrs. Munson does not seem unduly concerned." He gave up on getting comfortable and sat with his knees jackknifed up before him.

"Good."

"Jennie." His voice had taken on a new tone, a tone that augured a departure from banality.

I felt a rush of color to my cheeks and looked across the water. "What a beautiful day it is," I said in that trite, stupid way of a person ill at ease.

"Yes. Jennie—"

"Is all this your land?"

"As far as the eye can see. What I was going to—" He could not hold the jackknife position. He moved farther back on the rock, which helped the disposition of his legs but put his head twelve inches behind mine. He edged forward again.

"I wondered, as I do not see the hand of Capability Brown here."

"Jennie!"

His peremptory tone required that I adopt an expression of surprise. "What is it, Marndale? Is something the matter?"

He stood up once more and leaned down to me. "I made a wretched botch of it this morning. It isn't a companion for Jennie that I want. It is a wife."

"Your visit to the Munson twins has reminded you of your duty to the estate and title, I collect?"

One hand flailed the air futilely. "I don't want a son! Well—of course I want a son, but that is not what I am trying to say."

I adopted my schoolmistress's owl-like pose, for as the long-awaited moment approached, I found myself without a suitable expression to put on and did not wish to display my unbridled delight. "For goodness' sake, Marndale, what are you trying to say? It is not so difficult after all. You either want a son or you don't."

He reached out his two hands and drew me up from the rock. "I want a son, and I want a mother for Victoria, and most of all, I want a wife." His eyes burned into mine, and as he enumerated his wants his voice became husky.

"And you want these two ladies in one body?" I asked weakly.

"I want them in your body." He was still holding

on to both my hands. He released one, and his arm went around my waist.

"I have my own plans for this body, Marndale."

"I would not require all twenty-four hours of its time. Perhaps we can work out some mutually satisfactory arrangement." His other arm went around my shoulders in a disturbingly familiar way. A warbler, or perhaps it was a chiff-chaff, came to examine us with a glittering black eye, from the safety of a branch.

"What did you have in mind?"

He drew me insensibly closer, while his dark eyes hypnotized me into silence. "What I had in mind, Jennie, was—this," he whispered. His lips alit on mine, softly as a breeze. The gentleness of his kiss surprised me. I had anticipated something more in the nature of a ravishment. This filial touch scarcely warranted anything in the nature of a reciprocation on my part. He lifted his head and peeped down at my questioning face.

What he saw there gave him confidence, and soon I was being embraced much more satisfactorily. I have read somewhere that when a lobster is brought to the boil from cold water, he does not realize he is being cooked alive. The reason I mention boiling a lobster at this seemingly inappropriate time is that Marndale's attack was like that. He increased the heat of his embrace by insensible degrees till his lips were scalding mine.

I felt the touch of his jacket against me then gradually became aware of the firm wall of chest beneath it. All at the same time his lips moved on mine in such a distractingly delightful way that I forgot about his chest. I didn't notice it again until my ribs started to ache from the pressure of his arms. At no particular instant did my mind alert me to danger, but I realized at some point that he was crushing me against him so fiercely that I couldn't breathe. My lungs felt as if they would burst.

I made an ineffectual, token effort to release myself. This had the effect of increasing his ardor. When my head began to spin from a lack of air, I summoned all my strength and pushed him away. I was panting from the exertion—or perhaps from the sheer emotional exhaustion engendered by that embrace. In this breathless state speech was beyond me.

Marndale was made of sterner stuff. He blasted me with a smile of devastating intimacy and said, "I thought as much!"

"What on earth do you mean?" I panted out.

"Jennie Robsjohn, you are an imposter! An enchantress in prude's clothing. I have not only found myself a wife and mother, I have also got a schoolmistress and hostess and—mmmm." His head came closer as he enumerated my duties. That "mmmm" came from the throat, for his lips were on mine.

The chiff-chaff chirped his approval from the bough. The stream continued on its path toward the artistic serpentine of Capability Brown's devising. The trees basked in the glory of golden sunlight, and I found myself betrothed to Lord Marndale without his having asked the question or my having formally agreed to anything.

We walked home through the park arm-in-arm with his mount following. "I hope you are not in the habit of picking up strange ladies in inns, Charles?" I asked in that proprietary way of a lady who is sure of a satisfactory reply.

"My scheme at the time was only to make you Vickie's companion. I knew when I heard you lash out at me that you were the one to control her."

"You make her sound like a lion. She is docile as a lamb, when she is handled properly. She takes after her papa in that respect."

"I was not feeling so docile when Anselm landed in, claiming you as his long-lost friend."

"Then why did you bring him back?"

"He was an integral part of the working weekend. That job was to have been done in London. I only changed the venue because I was afraid you would either find yourself another beau or shear off on me completely. I invited Rita Pogue to keep Anselm in check." His quizzing smile held a hint of accusation.

"The coal scuttle was *not* my idea, Charles! I don't want you harping on that for the next thirty years."

"Whose idea was it that *I* was the gentleman she went calling on in the middle of the night?"

"That appeared to be a universal conclusion reached by us all. I understood she was a particular friend of yours." It was my turn to give a quizzing, accusing smile.

"Merely an acquaintance. One meets her everywhere." No stain of guilt colored his face. He was either an accomplished liar or innocent. I had fifty or so years, God willing, in which to determine the case, and if he was guilty, then I must put an end to such carrying on.

"I thought when you were so eager for me not to attend your dancing party that you required all your attention for Lady Pogue."

"No, no. That was to keep you from Anselm. I knew he was carrying on with Rita, but that was not to say he wouldn't snap up a wife if he met a lady his family would accept."

"And keeping me from Anselm was also the reason you gave permission for that untimely wilderness excursion?"

"But of course. I didn't want Anselm at you behind my back. When it rained all day, however, I was assailed by guilt, and decided to rescue you

185

from the bog. No—don't even think it! I did *not* know the woods were so wet. I hadn't been through them since last autumn, when they were perfectly passable."

Such was our conversation as we strolled at a leisurely pace. Had Marndale and I not come to an agreement, I would have been embarrassed to find Mrs. Irvine seated at her ease in the garden when she was supposed to be on the rack. To make matters worse, she jumped up when she saw us approaching and lit out for the back door with hardly a limp, though she did use a cane. Marndale called, and she stopped running.

"I am so happy to see you are feeling a little stouter, Mrs. Irvine," I smiled.

She examined me for signs of irony or anger. "The day was so fine I just hobbled out for a breath of air," she replied, with a simpering, apologetic smile at Marndale.

"You should not be standing on that ankle," he said, and led her back to her chair. We sat beside her in the rose garden.

"No, no, her shoulder was the excuse for remaining," I reminded him. "How is it, Mrs. Irvine?"

"Since I am revealed as a liar, I might as well admit it is fine, thank you very much." Her sharp eyes darted from Marndale to myself in a knowing way. "You two look about as merry as grigs in May. Is there something you want to tell me?"

"We are engaged," I told her. "I have captured Lord Marndale's heart."

"And a few other organs, from the sly grin on both your faces. Well, congratulations, Jennie. I didn't think you'd ever pull it—"

"Is Victoria back yet?" I asked hastily.

"Her rig rattled down the road five minutes ago. Have you settled on a date?"

"No," I said, too deep in love to think of such practical things.

"If you want me to attend, you must do it up soon and let me get back to Bath."

"You will be leaving us then, Mrs. Irvine?" Marndale asked. He had the grace to try for an air of disappointment.

"If there is one thing that sets my teeth on edge, it is being around lovers. They are intolerable for the first few weeks, till the thrill of it all wears thin. Then they become conversable again. I'll come back for a visit later on, if you'll have me."

"Don't wait till we have fallen out of love, or we shan't see you for a long, long time," he smiled.

Mrs. Irvine shook her head ruefully. "At least the house is big enough for me to get lost in. Aboard the *Prometheus* we did not have that luxury. We had to watch the moonlings making cow eyes at each other."

Victoria came running down the path, still in her bonnet. "I just passed a haywain on the main road, Papa!" she announced triumphantly. "It was as wide as a house. There was barely room for a mouse to get by, but I squeaked through without locking wheels or damaging the carriage. I have chosen the color I want to paint it, and—" She stopped chattering and just looked at us. "Why are you grinning? Papa, have you done it? Did she say yes?" she asked eagerly.

"Jennie has agreed to be my wife."

"Splendid! When can I have my twin brothers? I want to call them James and John, since Mrs. Munson has already used the names Peter and Paul."

"Twins?" Marndale exclaimed. "I will be happy with one boy. Two would be icing on the cake."

"Mrs. Irvine knows how to do it," Jennie said.

Mrs. Irvine turned a gimlet eye on me. "I trust

we are looking at a wait of at least nine months for this son!"

"Really, Mrs. Irvine!" I gasped.

"Nine and a half," Marndale said, unfazed. "It will take us two weeks to get the wedding prepared. Meanwhile, there will be no necessity for coal scuttles or any other foreign matter in our beds."

"Indeed there will not, for I'll lock her door and keep the key myself," Mrs. Irvine announced in a voice of sour triumph.

"There is always the window and a ladder. . . . " my fiancé said musingly.

"Marndale! Mrs. Irvine! For goodness' sake. Are you forgetting Victoria?"

Victoria gave a precocious shake of her head, as if to say, what am I to do with these unruly children? I recognized it well, for it was a habit she had picked up from me. "A little decorum, if you please," she said demurely. "I think this occasion calls for champagne. It will be served in the saloon in ten minutes. You will want to tidy your toilette, Jennie. Mama," she added, with a smile. "Do you mind if I call you so?"

I took her hand and we walked toward the house. "Strictly speaking, I will not be your mama until Marndale and I are married. However, I see no harm in practicing."

Marndale and Mrs. Irvine followed close behind us. I heard him say, "What was Vickie saying about twins?"

"Why, Marndale, I am surprised you don't know. What you have to do—"

I didn't bother trying to divert her. Enforcing social decorum was a job for a schoolmistress. I had to begin practicing the much freer manners of a marchioness.